"SHALL I REMOVE YOUR STOCKINGS?" MAC ASKED.

"No! No, I'll . . . I'll do it," Sterling insisted. But when she leaned forward, her spine creaked a protest louder than her own choked-back moan.

"What you'll do, Sterling, is lie down. Now, please." He removed her shoes and lifted her onto the bed, placing her head gently on the pillow. Then he sat down beside her and reached for the hem of her gown.

"Please, Mac. Don't."

"Just this once, allow someone to help you. That's what angels do. Will you let me?"

She closed her eyes, trying desperately to breathe evenly, so Mac wouldn't sense the wild fear his touch elicited. But as his fingertips moved up her legs to her hips, where he slowly peeled down her dark, filmy hose, she couldn't keep from trembling. It wasn't fear that was making her shiver, but desire.

"Mac?" Her voice sounded shaky, unfamiliar. "Mac, thank you. But I think it's time for you to go."

He picked up her feet and completed his task of removing the hose. He thoughtfully rubbed the delicate fabric between his fingers. "So sheer," he murmured. "It must be like wearing moonlight."

"Moonlight?"

He laughed. "I know, I'm hopelessly romantic about some things. Don't listen to me. I get punchy when I've overdosed on the company of a beautiful woman. Good night, Sterling." He leaned in and kissed her gently on the forehead. "Sweet dreams."

Long after he'd left she felt the heated circle his kiss had left, and the echo of his words. *Moonlight*. . . .

WHAT ARE *LOVESWEPT* ROMANCES?

They are stories of true romance and touching emotion. We believe those two very important ingredients are constants in our highly sensual and very believable stories in the LOVE-SWEPT line. Our goal is to give you, the reader, stories of consistently high quality that may sometimes make you laugh, sometimes make you cry, but are always fresh and creative and contain many delightful surprises within their pages.

Most romance fans read an enormous number of books. Those they truly love, they keep. Others may be traded with friends and soon forgotten. We hope that each LOVESWEPT romance will be a treasure—a "keeper." We will always try to publish

LOVE STORIES YOU'LL NEVER FORGET
BY AUTHORS YOU'LL ALWAYS REMEMBER

The Editors

Mac's Angels:
THE LAST DANCE

SANDRA CHASTAIN

BANTAM BOOKS
NEW YORK · TORONTO · LONDON · SYDNEY · AUCKLAND

MAC'S ANGELS: THE LAST DANCE
A Bantam Book / December 1998

LOVESWEPT and the wave design are registered trademarks of
Bantam Books, a division of Bantam Doubleday Dell Publishing Group,
Inc. Registered in U.S. Patent and Trademark Office and elsewhere.

ISBN 0-553-44666-5

Published simultaneously in the United States and Canada

Bantam Books are published by Bantam Books, a division of Bantam Dou-
bleday Dell Publishing Group, Inc. Its trademark, consisting of the words
"Bantam Books" and the portrayal of a rooster, is Registered in U.S.
Patent and Trademark Office and in other countries. Marca Registrada.
Bantam Books, 1540 Broadway, New York, New York 10036.

PRINTED IN THE UNITED STATES OF AMERICA

OPM   10 9 8 7 6 5 4 3 2 1

PROLOGUE

In the fifteen years since he'd created the sanctuary known as Shangri-la, Lincoln McAllister had rarely left the New Mexican mountain. No one was more surprised than he when he decided to attend the wedding of Rhett Butler Montana and Katie Carithers, his latest beneficiaries and good friends.

It had been late November when he'd called Conner Preston's assistant, Sterling, just to check on the wedding plans. During their conversation he had casually asked Sterling, "Are you going to the wedding?"

"Oh, no," she'd answered. "I can't. What about you?"

"I don't think so. You know I rarely leave New Mexico."

"And I rarely leave Virginia."

"But you're responsible for the wedding," he'd said. "If you hadn't called me asking for an angel to help Katie find a way to pay off the plantation debts, she and Montana might never have met."

"But it was you who solved the problem, Mac, just as you always do. You should go. Conner thinks that a Christmas wedding in Louisiana will be the event of the season," she'd said, almost wistfully. "And I'll expect you to call me and share every detail."

She was about to hang up. "Tell you what," he'd blurted out unexpectedly. "If you'll go, I'll go. You know, in all the years we've talked on the phone and through E-mail, I don't even know what you look like."

"Nor I you. That way we can each be whatever the other chooses."

"Please come, Sterling. And," he'd added, "save the last dance for me."

There'd been a long silence. "Perhaps." Her voice was soft and tight. "We'll see."

"Perhaps," he repeated to himself now, reliving the phone conversation he had with Sterling as if it were yesterday. Such an old-fashioned word. There were so many things he wondered about his friend's assistant, this Sterling who rarely went out. Well, *perhaps* he'd know soon. If she actually made it to the wedding.

But that possibility seemed more and more remote, he thought as he drove his rental car up River Road toward the plantation. He could fix everyone else's problems. But personal relationships weren't among his successful projects. He should be back in his office, and back in control of things.

Control was important. His assistant was capable, but thus far, Mac had never left him completely in charge of what was lovingly thought of as Angel Central. He shouldn't have left. He had his cell phone, though he genuinely hoped it wouldn't ring.

And then it did.

"Mac here."

"Mac," Raymond, his assistant, said, "you've got a problem."

Mac groaned. Not today. Not when he was about to meet the woman whose voice had helped him get through a lot of sleepless nights. "What is it?"

"It's Ms. Lindsey," he said. "She's in some kind of trouble."

Mac felt his chest tighten. "Sterling? What's wrong? Where is she?"

"At the New Orleans airport and she says she needs you."

ONE

The Louisiana airport was a madhouse. A tribe of errant elves sang carols by the front door. Ticket agents were all wearing Santa hats, but their "ho-ho-ho's" were growing a bit frazzled. The passenger in front of Sterling had already gotten a head start celebrating the holidays by overindulging in what he called "a bit of Christmas cheer."

"I'm sorry for the confusion, ma'am," the uniformed attendant pushing Sterling's wheelchair said. "Folks in New Orleans do like a celebration."

"So do I," she said, wondering where that response came from. The last celebration she'd been to was her college graduation party ten years before. It had been a long time since she'd encountered a crowd like this, except on television. "Is it always this wild and crowded?"

Her escort laughed. "This is nothing. You ought to see the traffic during Mardi Gras. We wouldn't be moving at all. There are times I wish my limo could sprout wings and fly."

"I appreciate the personal service, but I don't need any help with my chair. I get to work and anywhere else I want to go every day by myself." Although, there were few places she ever wanted to go, besides work.

"I'm sure you do, but I have orders from Mr. Preston. I am to meet you at the plane, get you to the limo and to the hotel safely. In fact, I'm yours for the entire weekend, Ms. Lindsey."

Sterling sighed. Her boss, Conner Preston, and his wife, Erica, were worse than fussy parents. As far as they were concerned, this trip was a headline event, and nothing was going to go wrong. Sterling Lindsey had not only left the office, she had left the state of Virginia. It took a wedding to do it, but the legendary Sterling was finally going to meet her friend the head angel, Lincoln McAllister—Mac.

"And I don't need a limo and a driver," Sterling argued. "It's not that I can't walk. I just can't walk far. If you could get me to the baggage area, I can claim my own chair and go anywhere I want."

"Yes, ma'am. We're headed that way."

Sterling eyed the travelers, some with armfuls of packages, some carrying tired children, but all wearing expressions of anticipation. A joyous but hectic time for a wedding. New chances, new beginnings. It took a lot to get her excited, but even she was beginning to feel the anticipation bubble up inside her.

How long had it been since she'd looked forward to anything except work? That was hard to answer. Getting out of the rehabilitation hospital? Starting a new job? Both had been difficult milestones she struggled to pass, but those events were long over. This was something new she eagerly awaited, and these new feelings felt good.

Sterling was pulled back to reality when the driver suddenly came to a quick stop as a wedge-shaped contingent of police officers followed by dark-suited men plowed through the crowd.

"Sorry," he said, "looks like VIPs from Washington. They're due in today."

Sterling stared at the mass of men in dark intimidating suits. "Must be someone important with all those bodyguards. Who is it?" she whispered.

"Senator March is coming home to honor his constituents with his semiannual visit. The one in the middle is March, the one wearing gray is his personal aide. The rest are Secret Service men and local escorts, the state police."

"He has more guards than the president. Is he that unpopular?"

"Pretty much. But it looks as if the state of Louisiana's loss will soon be our country's gain. March is the leading candidate for the presidential nomination."

At that moment a little girl standing to the side of Sterling's chair dropped a rolling toy. She darted forward, bringing the throng of men to a halt. The man in the gray suit, March's personal aide, reached down, picked up the toy and the child, then with a reassuring smile returned her to her mother. As his eyes swept the crowd his gaze met Sterling's, and for one long moment locked there. His smile faded.

Sterling gasped.

She felt the air rush from her lungs. Everything around her—the airport, tourists, the sounds of Christmas cheer—disappeared. She was suddenly in some kind of vacuum, a time warp that sucked her back into the past.

Oh God. Please, no!

She'd seen those eyes before. They belonged to the man who'd sent her to hell, the man who put her in this wheelchair.

He blinked twice and frowned.

The mother took the child. Senator March flashed his best campaigning smile and held out his hand. The mother shook it then watched the entourage of bodyguards regroup and sweep the senator and his aide rapidly down the concourse. Sterling's attendant moved forward once more, falling in behind.

It was him. It had to be. She'd never forgotten those cold grayish-blue eyes, a color she'd never seen before or since. He hadn't been wearing a suit the last time she saw him, and he hadn't been smiling. He'd been wearing a loose ski mask, revealing only his eyes and mouth, and he'd been on the other end of the gun that shot her, a terrifying smirk on his face. With a single bullet, he'd changed her life.

Sterling's mind raced in all directions. Everything blurred into a dizzying mass of color. She could hardly breathe and her heart beat heavily from the struggle. She felt as if she were going to faint. What should she do?

The chair moved forward. Ahead, the passageway slanted slightly up and Sterling could see the senator's party. Her eyes were riveted on the man in the gray suit. As if he knew she was watching, he turned and looked at her.

He grinned.

He remembered her.

After whispering something in the senator's ear, he moved smoothly out of formation. Once free, he walked rapidly in her direction, fighting against the horde of travelers.

Sterling started to panic. She would call the police. No, the people guarding him were police officers. She'd call someone at the office. That was no good either. Conner was at Montana's groomsmen's luncheon and Katie was being entertained by her bridesmaids. Here she was, trapped in a wheelchair, in a crowded airport with the man who'd shot her ten years ago heading directly for her. She had to get away. And she didn't have much time.

"Wait!" she said to her earnest helper.

"Why? Did you leave something on the plane?"

"No, I need to—to go to the ladies' room, please."

"Certainly. But I can't go with you," he said.

"You don't have to. I'm accustomed to looking after myself."

At the entrance, Sterling took over, wheeling herself into the handicapped stall. *What now? He'll be waiting for me when I come out. I can't run.*

Helplessly, she looked around. It had taken ten years for her to get her life back in order. *Ten years.* Now, when she'd finally conquered her fear of the outside world and taken a chance, this happened. Her hands trembled and she couldn't breathe.

No! No! I might have been an innocent bystander when you robbed and murdered an old man who meant you no harm, but this time I'm ready for you. You bastard, you're not going to get to me!

She forced herself to breathe, in—out. In—out. She had to escape, call someone. She had to stay calm and think fast.

Finally the answer came to her. *I can't run but I can walk.* Chances are, if he read the newspaper stories he won't know that. The press had focused only on the tragedy. WOMAN UNCONSCIOUS. CRITICAL. MAY NEVER WALK AGAIN. After months in the hospital, with no progress made in finding the killer, her story had died in the wake of the next crime. Obviously, he'd thought he was safe.

From the small bag she was holding, Sterling removed and donned a scarf that covered her dark brown hair. Next she pulled on the jacket she had draped across her lap, gritted her teeth, and stood.

The pain hit her instantly.

You can do this, Sterling. One step at a time.

Opening the stall door, she peered out. Once the passageway was clear, she closed the door, leaving the chair inside, and made her way slowly to the exit. The limo driver was her first test. She straightened her shoulders, blended into a group of women leaving the ladies' room and walked right past him into the flow of travelers. He never even noticed her.

The pain intensified with every step. She wasn't going to be able to walk to the exit, at least not without stopping. Best that she find a place to rest. A restaurant—no, a bar. A bar would be darker. She could hide there.

Desperately, she looked ahead. She couldn't see a safe place nearby. She needed a better disguise. Anxiously, her gaze swept back and forth, fearing that she'd see her stalker. And then she did, just in time to turn her head. He walked past her.

She'd escaped for now, but she knew it was only for the moment. By announcing an imagined threat on the senator's life, he could amass an army of searchers. At the next lobby she turned into a ladies' shop. Ten minutes later she emerged, wearing a ski sweater with a fur hood that covered her hair and black-tinted glasses that hid part of her face. Even that disguise wouldn't last long.

By the time she made her way painfully back to the concourse, it was swarming with police officers.

Just walk on, Sterling.

But this time her body wasn't responding. She'd reached the end of her endurance. Every step was sheer torture, and she'd begun to falter. Thank God, a bar was just a few steps away.

She stumbled inside and took a seat in the

corner. She ordered a drink and sipped it slowly. Then a second, explaining to the waiter that she was lingering at the bar because she had time to kill between flights.

"Going skiing, are you?" the waiter asked, eyeing her fur hood.

"Yes, yes, I am." She'd made a poor choice, she decided. She was in Louisiana, not Colorado. But it was too late to change her disguise now.

Ten o'clock. She'd been in the bar nearly an hour when she looked up and saw her hunter in the doorway. He hadn't seen her yet, but he was headed toward her.

Just before she started to panic he turned away, giving her time to stand and move past him. Slowly, but not too slowly, she made her way toward the door and into the corridor. At the ladies' room she paused and ducked inside, where she sank down onto one of the toilet seats. By now the limo driver would have informed Conner that she was missing. Without knowing the danger of doing so, he might contact the police. And the police were working with the man who'd shot her. She was totally screwed.

It was obvious she wasn't going to get out of the airport undiscovered. She was physically exhausted and in such pain that she couldn't trust her legs to walk any farther. She had to find some help.

If only . . .

Mac. Maybe she could reach Mac. Mac could tell her what to do. That's what Lincoln McAllister did—fix things and people. Angel Central had helped so many people in trouble. Mac was the head angel and right now she needed an angel, desperately.

Gritting her teeth, she forced herself to stand. Why had she turned away all those telemarketers trying to sell her a portable phone? Because she'd never expected to be away from her regular one.

There are phones at the next gate, Sterling. You can do it. Slowly, step by painful step, she made her way down the concourse toward the bank of phones against the wall. Change. She needed change. Quarters. She fed coins into the machine.

"Shangri-la," the voice said. "How may we help you?"

"Yes, I need to speak with Lincoln McAllister."

"I'm sorry, he's away. May I take a message?"

Sterling felt a fresh wave of fear. She couldn't see the killer, but he couldn't be far. Mac was away. Of course he was away, he was on his way here. "I'm at the New Orleans airport. This is an emergency. Please—please tell him that Sterling needs him."

"Sterling? Hold on a minute."

It was less than a minute later that Mac's familiar voice came on the line. "Are you all right?"

"Yes. But I'm in big trouble."

"Are you in danger?"

"Yes. Someone's . . . after me. They are all . . . searching for me."

"Where are you?"

"I'm still in the airport. Gate seven."

"Look around. How far are you from the nearest restaurant?"

She turned casually to look. "I can't see one, except for a food court and that's too open. There's a bar. I was just there."

"Can you get back to the bar? Stay in a public place until I get there?"

"I can make it. How long will that take?"

"I'm approaching the airport now."

"How?"

"My plane landed a half hour ago and I rented a car for the drive to Carithers's Chance. I can be back there in fifteen minutes."

"Hurry, Mac. And don't tell anyone—not even Conner."

He didn't ask questions, nor did he argue. Conner already knew. Mac had his office alert Conner the minute they told him that Sterling was calling. Just as he was hanging up, he added, "Ah, Sterling, it just occurred to me. I feel like I know you. We've talked on the phone for years, but how will I recognize you?"

She felt a smile curl her lips. "I'm the only fool wearing a fur-lined hood and tinted glasses in New Orleans."

He laughed. "Lose the glasses, Sterling, and wait for me. And Sterling, if anyone threatens you, start screaming and don't stop."

❖―――❖

Sterling sat in the other corner of the bar, hiding behind the server's stand, slowly sipping lukewarm coffee. Her eyes were tightly focused on the doorway. She'd identified herself to Mac, but he'd failed to give her a description of himself.

How would she know him?

Would he arrive before the police returned? Sterling wouldn't think about what might happen if he didn't. For more than a year after she'd been shot, she'd relived that horrible morning when a lone gunman had entered the office of Commonwealth Securities, killed her boss, a senior partner, and then shot her in the back.

She'd been in the copy room, printing and collating brochures about a new stock offering. Arms full of brochures, she'd backed into his office, straight into the robber. Mr. Eldon was lying on the floor, bleeding to death, and his killer was emptying the safe. He turned a gun on her. And then she saw those cold eyes, the eyes of a murderer. When she screamed and whirled to run for help, he swore and pulled the trigger. As she'd lost consciousness the imprint of those hard, blue-gray eyes had etched themselves forever in her brain and eventually her nightmares.

They never caught him. The bearer bonds he'd stolen were unmarked and never recovered. And Sterling was left unconscious with a bullet lodged dangerously near her spine.

Now, ten years later, the fear and pain had returned. The man who'd shot her had become a senator's aide, possibly in a position to influence national policy. A murderer was the assistant to a man headed for the presidency? He'd killed a man ten years ago. What would he do to protect the life he'd built? She didn't want to consider the possibilities.

A glance at her watch told her that fifteen minutes had passed.

What if Mac didn't come?

But he did. Striding into the bar, a man wearing a baseball cap and a leather bomber's jacket stopped in the center and looked around, and then he saw Sterling. With a quick nod, he slid into the booth beside her. "I'm Mac."

"Yes." You certainly are, she wanted to say, but didn't. "I'm Sterling."

Compact, with a nose that might have been broken once, Lincoln McAllister was nothing like Sterling expected.

He was much more.

His deep, calm voice was deceptive, designating only the persona he created for the public. She would have recognized that voice anywhere. It didn't match the man.

But neither did the lifestyle she knew he lived. His clothes were casual, yet expensive. His hair, a dark blond, was showing hints of silver at the edges. It was thick and long, curling to the collar of his blue denim shirt. Everything about him spoke of power. He was like some old-world warrior ready to do battle in an arena.

"Sterling," he was saying. "Listen to me. We

have to move quickly. I saw the suits searching the airport for you. They're not even trying to hide their efforts."

It was obvious that he didn't know. She wanted to explain her problem to him, but all she could do was stare. She must look like an animal, frozen in the headlights of an oncoming car. "Mac, I . . ."

"Don't try to explain. Right now I don't care why they're looking for you. We have to get you out of here without giving them a chance to take you into 'protective' custody."

She nodded approvingly, grateful and relieved that Mac was by her side.

"Now, here's what we're going to do. You and I are going to the private area of the airport. My plane is refueling and getting ready for takeoff. We'll tell them we're flying home to Aspen for the holidays. All we have to do is walk down the concourse into the private area and board my plane. They won't be expecting that."

She nodded again.

"All right, let's go. We don't want to look rushed, but we'd better hurry."

Sterling swallowed hard. Hurry? "I—I can't, Mac."

"Why not? Are you hurt?"

"No, that's not it."

"Then we have to go. Now." He stood.

"Mac, you don't understand. I—I can't walk. Not anymore. I need my wheelchair from baggage claim."

He sat back down, a confused look on his face. "You can't walk?"

"I can, a little, but only for short periods of time. I've had to walk so much in the last hour that my legs are . . . used up. I'll never make it."

He furrowed his brow in thought. "All right," he finally said. "If you need transportation, you've got it." He ripped off her fur-lined hood, removed his baseball cap, crammed it on her head, then handed her his coat. "That fur is too visible. Wear my cap and stuff this jacket under your sweater. You're pregnant and you don't feel well."

Sterling followed his instructions, glad that her sweater was oversized.

Before she knew what was happening, Mac scooped her up and moved quickly through the bar, flagging down one of the motorized vehicles used to carry passengers down the concourse. "Sit here with these folks, darling," he said, depositing her next to an elderly couple. "She's all right," he assured them. "She's just a little queasy. Don't know why her morning sickness comes in the afternoon."

Mac sat beside her and motioned for the driver to move on. "Thanks for sharing your ride," he said, giving the elderly couple a wide smile. "We've just got to get home for Christmas. The children are waiting."

"Oh, you poor thing," the older woman said, patting Sterling on the knee. "How many do you have now?"

"One—" Sterling said, ready to strangle Mac.

"Three—" Mac said at the same time, quickly coming up with names of people he knew. "A little girl—Erica. Erica is just a year old and she's going to look just like her mother. And twin boys, Conner and Rhett. They'll be three next month."

"My—my, three children with one on the way, and you're so young. What's this one going to be? Or don't you know yet?"

"Do we know yet?" she asked Mac, a hint of amusement in her voice.

"No." He grinned, surprised at how much he was enjoying the exchange with Sterling in the midst of danger. He only hoped the elderly couple's eyesight was poor. No pregnancy he'd ever seen had quite the contours of Sterling's sweater. "We like to be surprised. But we're hoping for another girl. Aren't we, darling?"

If he'd been surprised at the lighthearted banter, he was even more surprised at himself when he slid his arm around her shoulders and pulled her close for a quick kiss that was intended to be a husband's mark of assurance.

The moment his lips touched her cheek, his pulse raced.

Startled by his unexpected physical response, he pulled back, masking his confusion by looking around. Could it be the threat of danger that made a shiver ripple down his spine?

"You okay, Dad?" Sterling asked. "Don't tell me you're going to get sick too." She flashed the couple a motherly smile. "Every time I get pregnant, he throws up."

"It's a whole new world, isn't it?" the man said. "In my day men didn't get involved in having the children. It was the woman's job; we just supported them."

"That's what I keep telling Barney," Sterling said. "But he likes being a house husband. That way he can do his quilt designs without the men at the gym teasing him."

The old man's mouth fell open. "You make quilts?"

"Oh, sure," Mac said, his humor fading a bit. "While preparing for my next fight. Calms my nerves and, truthfully, the quilting designs bring in as much money as my boxing matches."

"Can't we go any faster?" he asked the driver of the vehicle.

"And what do you do, dear?" the old woman asked Sterling.

At that moment Sterling saw the man in the gray suit and his expanded number of escorts moving through the crowd, stopping everyone. Behind them, her boss, Conner Preston, raced down the concourse, giving a great imitation of a passenger about to miss his flight. What was he doing here?

Sterling's heart sank when she saw the waiter from the bar being rushed toward the man in the gray suit. They talked briefly for a moment, then the aide touched his head and extended his hand as if he were giving an urgent order.

"Darling," Sterling said, "I think we'd better hurry. I feel a little odd." She touched her stomach and bent over, whispering, "The real Conner's here. How'd he know?"

"I told my office to call him," Mac said under his breath, then more loudly, "You can't have the baby here, darling. We're almost at our gate."

Mac had seen Conner and Conner had just seen them. Though how he managed to get here when he was supposed to be at a luncheon, she couldn't imagine. He came to a sudden stop and engaged the senator's aide in conversation. The conversation became heated. Conner suddenly drew back and belted the aide. Instantly, the guards surrounded Conner, turning their backs on the tram.

The tram came to a quick stop. Mac lifted Sterling out of the car and dashed down a corridor, leaving the old man and his wife in stunned disbelief.

"Sorry," Mac called behind. "We have to hurry. We're having our baby at home. In—Aspen."

"Aspen?" Sterling repeated, breathless from being in his arms. "I'm sorry, Mac. But Aspen?"

"Sure," he said, pushing through the double doors and past a desk where two pilots were studying charts. "What's wrong with Aspen? I like snow, don't you?"

"Not a bit."

He moved through another set of doors, then nodded at an employee at the foot of the steps leading up to a sleek silver jet. "Fine, once the baby comes, we'll move to Hawaii."

There was no sign of the policemen, but Sterling knew it was only a matter of minutes before they'd show up. She tried to hide her fear by keeping with the silly conversation Mac had started.

"Okay, Mac. Hawaii, it is."

Mac climbed the stairs without a hint of strain. "Close the doors, John. Let's get out of here while we can. The posse is right behind us."

"Yes, sir, Mr. McAllister."

By the time Mac had deposited Sterling in one of the luxurious leather seats, the plane was taxiing across the tarmac, headed toward the runway.

"Are you all right?" Mac asked Sterling.

"Well, my stomach has settled down, but I'm having trouble with this 'baby' poking into my ribs. I think his skin is made of leather."

"Complaints, complaints, that's the way with you pregnant women. Here, let me fasten your seat belt."

She could have done it herself, but for now she was content to let him help her. Until he leaned forward and reached for the belt behind her. Big mistake. Her body felt as if *it* were the object taking off into the sky and not the plane.

"Mac, if you'll let me deliver our . . . baby first, it'll be easier."

"My mama told me that I should never take the easy way out." He pulled the long end from beneath her bottom, snapped it into the buckle, then adjusted the location of the belt.

"Mine too. But she also said if you want a thing done right, you'd better do it yourself."

"And everyone knows that Sterling Lindsey is a do-it-herself, in-charge-of-her-fate woman, don't they?"

"Yes, she is." Sterling caught his hand and held it for a moment. "Mac, thank you. You probably saved my life."

"Don't thank me yet. We're not off the ground."

She was much too close, too trusting, and as his mother might have said, he was treading in shark-infested waters. Helping people was one thing. But this was different. This was rapidly becoming personal. And his record with women he cared about was so bad that he'd sworn never to become emotionally involved with one again.

Mac leaned back, removing his hand from Sterling's. "Are we cleared for takeoff, John?" he called out to the pilot.

"Yes, sir. Just delaying till you got aboard."

"Then get us moving before they have time to stop us."

"Sure thing, sir."

The engines climbed to a steady roar and the plane moved forward. Once they were airborne, Mac moved to the cockpit to confer with the pilot.

Sterling pulled the jacket from beneath her sweater. There was no longer a need for a disguise. No more family hurrying home for Christmas. No more little girl and no more twins. She let out a sigh. The fantasy had been fun—for a while.

Mac soon returned and sat down beside her. "All right, I'm ready to listen. Who is the man in the gray suit?"

TWO

The time had come for Sterling to tell Mac the truth.

"Give me a minute," she said as she leaned back in her seat and closed her eyes. Every bone in her body ached. But it wasn't physical pain that paralyzed her now; it was the emotional anguish that drained the movement from her body. She didn't ask where they were going or how Mac intended to get away. All she cared about was that for now she was safe.

As if he understood her mental exhaustion, Mac didn't press her. Instead, she heard him rise once more and walk over to the cockpit, to have a quiet conversation with the pilot. Moments later she heard the clatter of glass hit the counter. A door—a cabinet opened and closed. Then footsteps.

"Sterling? Drink this."

She opened her eyes.

Mac was sitting beside her, holding out a glass of burgundy liquid. "It's whiskey."

"Oh, I'm not much on hard liquor."

"This is medicinal, not social. Drink it, Sterling."

She sat up straight, accepted the glass, and took a reluctant sip. With a grimace she swallowed it and forced herself to take more. The whiskey acted as a warming agent, accelerating her heartbeat and calming her nerves. With two more sips she emptied the glass and handed it to Mac.

"I'm sorry, Mac. I'm taking you away from the wedding and putting you in danger. If you'll just get me on a plane for Virginia, I'd appreciate it. I knew I shouldn't have come."

Then why did you? He wanted to ask. It would have been nice if she'd come because she was just a little curious about him.

Sterling's gaze darted away from his, as if she was as uncomfortable about seeing him in person as he was right now. The paleness of her skin and the tight expression she'd drawn on her face truly worried him. She wasn't as strong as she pretended to be and he very much wanted to protect her and not scare her away.

In spite of the fact Sterling was on first name-basis with half the powerful people in the Western world, Mac believed that she really didn't leave her office. What was happening to her now had to be a big surprise.

For Mac, her need for a wheelchair was an even

bigger one. Conner had never once mentioned Sterling's handicap. It had seemed odd when Conner arranged for her to have living quarters in the building where Paradox, Inc. was located, but Mac too lived where he worked, so it didn't seem out of the ordinary. Conner gave Sterling a beachside apartment in Virginia Beach, one that was attached to the headquarters and easily accessible to her office.

What Mac didn't understand was that Conner never explained why he'd gone through the trouble of creating an apartment for her there. He could only assume that the danger, the chair, and her isolation were connected. Conner was a man with a big heart. If Sterling couldn't walk on the beach, it would be just like Conner to give her a balcony from which she would enjoy the ocean breezes and the sun.

But there was no evidence that she'd made use of that sunlight. Her skin was much too milky white. She removed the baseball cap from her head, allowing a mass of dark brown hair to fall over her shoulders and down her back, a casual look that Mac doubted many ever saw.

What *had* convinced her to come to the wedding? He knew she'd had other invitations to special events, and they apparently hadn't drawn her out of her safe, well-organized world. Not even Conner and Erica's wedding had enticed her. But she'd left Virginia and flown to New Orleans for this one. Perhaps—there it was, Sterling's own soft-spoken word that so intrigued him—*Perhaps* I'll come, she'd said. We'll see.

Suddenly it all became clear. He'd challenged her to come. And she had. He'd brought her into danger because he'd wanted to meet her. And now he had the responsibility of removing her from that danger. Nothing new about that. He'd spent the last half of his life trying to rectify problems for others. So far his success rate had been pretty good, for acquaintances and strangers.

In order to succeed with Sterling, he had to maintain that distance. He couldn't let this become personal. Personal failure had isolated Mac almost as much as Sterling's chair had isolated her. They were two of a kind. That was not a reassuring thought.

As he watched, Sterling seemed to fade visibly. He had to revive her if he were going to find the answers he needed. What was that she'd called him. Barney. He smiled, assuming that she was referring to the Rubbles, not the dinosaur. Barney . . . what was Barney's wife's name. He ought to know.

Bingo. Betty.

"Er . . . Don't worry about missing the wedding, Betty, a wedding's no big deal. I'm just worried about . . . about little Conner and Rhett and Erica. They'll be so disappointed. We did promise them some wedding cake, didn't we?"

Her eyelids flew open.

She had cat eyes—green, with little flecks of brown that matched her hair. Where they'd been veiled and calm earlier, a liveliness now came rushing back.

"Betty?" she asked.

"Why not? Barney is married to Betty, isn't he? I don't watch cartoons but I seem to remember *The Flintstones.*"

Mac tried to maintain the serious look he was always accused of having. This ongoing exchange of quips was something new. He wasn't quite certain of its result. He'd never made small talk with a woman. Now, leaning forward, he surprised himself further as he threaded his fingers through hers and laid her hand across her stomach. "And think of the baby."

"Lincoln McAllister, if I didn't know better, I'd *think* it was you who got pounded in a fistfight at the terminal, not Conner."

"I suppose we'll just have to let them all grow up and get married. They can have their own cake."

Now that he had her relaxed and talking, he voiced the question he had to have answered. "Who is he, Sterling?"

"Who?" she asked. *You sound incredibly stupid, Sterling. You're feeling a man's hand on your body and your mind is turning to mush.*

"The man who was searching the airport, looking for you."

"I don't know his name," she said, putting aside the fun and games. "I just know he's a murderer. And unless you get away from me, he'll come after you too."

"I'm sure he will. He didn't look like the kind of

man to take no for an answer. But you didn't answer my question. Why is the man in the gray suit after you?"

She took a deep breath.

Mac squeezed her hand. "Tell me, Sterling."

She nodded. If Mac was anything like the powerful men in her past, he wouldn't believe her, but she'd tell him anyway. It might be the only way he could save his own life. Hers? She wasn't at all certain that was possible anymore.

"The last time I saw him was a decade ago. I was an intern in an investment firm. The man I worked for had just landed a new client. Some kind of reclusive Howard Hughes type. He was very mysterious, insisting on setting up an appointment at lunchtime when the office was supposed to be empty."

"How'd you get involved?"

"If I hadn't been such a klutz, I'd have been gone. I was in the copy room, trying to run off and collate some brochures about a new stock offering. Mr. Eldon wanted it ready to show to his new client, in case he was interested in additional investments. But I couldn't get the machine to work right and I was running late."

She paused, flashing back to that day in her mind. She had been so young then, so full of drive and ambition. Sterling Lindsey had successfully completed her classes at William and Mary. The big city of Philadelphia would, if the internship with the small but prestigious investment firm worked out, be her new home.

Assisting the senior partner in the office was her assignment. She hadn't known then that Mr. Eldon was easing his way to retirement, that his client list had shrunk to the point where he was merely a figurehead, and that her internship would be less challenging than working in the mailroom. Sterling thought he was a kind and caring man, willing to teach her about the business. To complete the future she'd planned, she was engaged to an up-and-coming financial planner who was working on his MBA. Once her internship was complete, the two of them would be ready to take on the world.

Until that fateful day.

Mr. Eldon had been extremely anxious and fidgety. He explained that the amount of money involved in this deal was staggering. The phone call from the well-known, reclusive millionaire came from out of the blue. He wanted to buy bearer bonds and had insisted the transaction be handled in the office rather than at the bank. His reputation for avoiding the public eye was common knowledge, so there was no reason to doubt his request for privacy and for the unmarked bonds.

The partners were surprised. Though Mr. Eldon had once been very successful, years had passed since he'd brought a large amount of money into the firm. He'd been relegated to researching and preparing brochures. This sale would be considered a coup. Mr. Eldon would regain respect. His prestige would be restored.

By the time Sterling ran off the pages for the

prospectus and collated them, her lunch hour had already begun. Frantically, she got the last pages into the spiral binding and returned to Mr. Eldon's office, glancing at the wall clock.

"Oops!" She'd really let the time get away. She should have finished thirty minutes ago. It was time for Mr. Eldon's appointment. She dashed down the inside connecting corridor. The office next door was empty. She and Mr. Eldon were the only ones left on their end of the hall. Sterling felt a knot in her stomach. She'd better hurry.

She twisted the knob on the rear door to Mr. Eldon's office and backed inside, turning as she entered. "I'm sorry. It took longer than I thought to . . ." It wasn't Mr. Eldon kneeling in front of the safe. It was a tall man in jeans and a pullover shirt. Over his face he wore a loose-fitting ski mask with holes cut for his eyes and mouth. At Sterling's entrance he sprang to his feet, turned, and pointed a revolver straight at her.

"Don't move!"

With his cold gray-blue gaze riveted on her, she couldn't have moved if she'd wanted to. Holding the gun at arm's length away, he knelt and finished emptying the bonds out of the safe sliding them into a brief case.

Beside the desk, Sterling could see Mr. Eldon on the floor, his blood pooling outward from his body. He wasn't moving. He'd die if she didn't get help. She made a move toward him.

"I told you to stand still, unless you want to join the old man."

Voices down the hallway drew the thief's attention. "Somebody get the police. It's Smitty, the security guard. He's been hurt," a voice called out. The sound of running feet moved past the outer door.

The thief stood, fastened his case, and started toward the door. He'd shot Mr. Eldon. He was about to escape. She had to stop him.

"Help," Sterling screamed, flung the stack of prospectuses toward the killer, and whirled around.

Later she remembered that she'd heard the sound of gunfire. Her body jerked and she collapsed crazily, but she felt nothing. Only the sensation of falling. And then everything went black.

That had been the beginning of many days of darkness, of a deep void that had surrounded and consumed her.

"And the man?" Mac said softly, drawing her back to the present. He still held her hand, and she clasped his tightly in return. "He was the man in the airport, Sterling, the one in the gray suit?"

"Yes, Senator March's aide. He's the thief. He's the man who killed Mr. Eldon. He's the man who shot me."

"Whoa!" Mac let out a deep breath. "This is pretty serious stuff. You're telling me the senator's aide is a murderer?"

"He wasn't the senator's aide back then. Well, he might have been. I don't know. Nobody got a look at him but me, and I was unconscious for a long time. When I came out of it, I couldn't give them a good enough description, except for the eyes, and there were no fingerprints."

"How can you be so certain now?"

Sterling jerked her hand away from Mac's grip. It was beginning all over again. The questions. The disbelief. "His eyes. They were this close—" She held out her hands, measuring twelve inches between them. "I'd never forget."

"He was alone?"

"So far as I know."

"How much money did he get?"

"Over a million dollars in unregistered bearer bonds. They were never recovered and he was never found."

Mac nodded. "So the thief became the millionaire he pretended to be, got away with murder, and left you . . . injured."

"He left me paralyzed. When I fell I hit my head. They never knew whether or not that caused the coma, but I couldn't remember anything for months. The press had a field day. The only witness, me, suffered from amnesia and paralysis."

"Of course the real millionaire never contacted your boss in the first place," Mac said.

"No. It was all an elaborate hoax. Mr. Eldon knew, even if I didn't, that keeping the bonds in his office was forbidden. But he needed, wanted to prove he was still as good as the other partners. And he took a chance that got him killed."

"What about the security guard in the building—Smitty?"

"Smitty never saw what hit him. Mr. Eldon was dead, and I was in the hospital for over a year. Even though I was only an intern, the firm was still forced to pay my expenses. All the newspapers made me front-page news—for a while. Surely you heard about it. Everybody else in the world did."

"I seem to remember reading the story," Mac said. "I should have followed up on your situation. Maybe I could have helped you."

"Nobody could have helped. They even suspected that I was involved. That and my long illness cost me my future as a financial planner."

Mac lifted his eyes in question. "They thought you were involved?"

"Yes. I wasn't, but the police never quite believed me. They kept a check on me for years. It took a long time for me to take control of my life again, to find another job. If it hadn't been for Conner . . ."

"Conner never mentioned how you came to work for him."

"He came to the rehabilitation center to see one of his army buddies, who worked out at the station next to me. We talked and he offered me a job. I wasn't certain I could live away from the hospital. He convinced me that I could. Now I guess I'll be back to square one again. Unemployed."

"Sterling, Conner won't fire you over this."

"No, he won't. But I'll have to move. Either that or the senator's aide will find me. I still have a bullet lodged near my spine as a reminder of the first time he got to me. The next time he does, I won't be able to get away."

"Maybe—maybe you're overreacting," he suggested. "Why would he think you can identify him now?"

She shot a quick accusing glance at him. "He knows, or at least he suspects. Otherwise, why the search?"

He nodded. "Even if we're wrong, we have to assume that you're in danger. It's a good thing my plane was already gassed up for the return trip. We might not have been allowed to leave the airport."

"Airport! What about Conner?" Sterling asked. "He deliberately hit that man. What will they do to him?"

"Conner can take care of himself," Mac said absentmindedly. "We have to figure out what we're going to do about you."

"I'll go to the police if that's what I have to do to save Conner."

"And say what? That the leading presidential candidate's trusted adviser is a murderer and a thief? I don't think they'd buy it. Besides, we don't know who we can trust."

"What about the press? I'll admit I don't look forward to being headline news again, but if that's what it takes . . ."

"Not yet, Sterling. Let's not make any decisions until we get a little more information."

She let out a sigh of relief. "Thank you, Mac. I'm

not usually a coward, but you have no idea what the press can do to you."

He could have told her he knew. Long ago he'd discovered that sad truth for himself. But that was a road he didn't want to go down—not today.

"I don't think the senator's aide will release this to the press and I doubt March knows the truth. For now, we'll just leave him in the dark. We have some serious planning to do—away from here."

"Mac, there isn't anywhere far enough away that a government official can't reach. Once you put me on this plane, your life was changed forever."

"My, we're being pretty pessimistic, aren't we? You know what they call me, I'm the head angel. I have friends in high places. Cheer up. Barney Rubble's baby won't be born in prison."

"Mac, stop it. I know you're only trying to get my mind off the gravity of the situation. But please don't joke about having children. It isn't funny."

Apparently his attempt at relieving the tension with levity had touched a sore spot.

"I'm sorry. I'm only trying to keep your spirits up. I never meant to cause you pain."

Sterling stretched her shoulders. "If you really want to do something for me, you'll get me home to my hot tub."

"Good idea. One hot tub coming up," he said, "but it won't be at your place. You're right about one thing." He studied her seriously. "I'm sorry, but you can't go home again. I think it's time you got personally acquainted with Shangri-la."

Shangri-la. Sterling knew about Mac's hideaway in the mountains of New Mexico. Conner had spent time there, recovering from the wounds he received in Berlin when his brother was killed. Conner wasn't the first. Mac had his own private medical facility. Anyone he helped was safe and welcome there, for as long as necessary. That's where Mac had lived for all the years Sterling had known of him.

"Will your family be there?" she asked curiously.

That question caught him off guard. "Family?"

"You said you watched *The Flintstones*. I assume that means you have children."

"I have a daughter. But she doesn't have any contact with our guests."

"And your wife?" Sterling was being uncharacteristically direct. Mac's personal life was none of her business. She couldn't imagine what had come over her.

"I lost my wife, fifteen years ago."

"Oh, I'm sorry. I didn't mean to pry."

It seemed natural that she should reach out and touch him, share the pain she saw in his eyes. She hadn't expected the feeling of protectiveness that swept over her when she did. As they looked at each other, for one electric moment everything seemed to stop.

"It's all right," he muttered. "I've asked you some pretty hard questions. Now it's your turn to ask me."

"No. Your family is private. Your helping me—is different. I mean . . . that's what you do, isn't it? I know you helped Conner and Erica. And Katie Carithers. And there was that football player, too, a friend of Conner's. I'll be glad to pay you."

"Sterling, I never helped any of them personally. I have people, on my staff, outsiders who've been helped in the past. They do the real work. Not me. I'm just the connection, the arranger. I'm not someone you'd want to depend on."

"Yes, you are, Lincoln McAllister. You're exactly the man I'd want to depend on. But—" She pulled back, reminding herself that she could get him killed, that she'd sworn to protect herself alone. "Because of me, Conner might be in jail. I've probably spoiled Katie and Montana's wedding, and I've put you at risk."

"Yep, you're a dangerous woman, Sterling Lindsey. And you're brave and you're beautiful. And I'm taking you home to meet Jessie."

"Who's Jessie?"

"Jessie is the woman I love most in this world."

Conner Preston sat sprawled in a straight-backed chair, presenting the illusion of total relaxation, a pose that was just that—an illusion.

"I told you, my name is Conner Preston."

"And do you normally interfere with a police action?"

"No, but I was trained as a Green Beret. When I saw you, I thought you were a hijacker and I reacted automatically."

The man in the gray suit rubbed his cheek and frowned, not yet ready to accept Conner's explanation.

"You know who I am," Conner said. "How about telling me who you are?"

The man in the gray suit looked startled, as if he expected everyone to know him. Conner bit back a smile. What an inflated ego, he thought.

He finally answered. "My name is Vincent Dawson."

"Sorry, Vince, but"—Conner rubbed his neck—"you only got a black eye. Your guys almost broke my neck."

"You're lucky they didn't."

"So, who were you going after out there?"

The man leaned casually against the wall of the small airport security room. But his eyes belied his movement. Conner decided this was a man who never relaxed. Men like him always had something to hide. Conner wondered what his secret was.

"Doesn't matter, Mr. Preston. It's none of your concern. I think I'm going to let you go. For now. Next time stay out of something that isn't your affair. That's the way people get killed."

"Sure." Conner watched him leave the room. Vincent had just issued a veiled threat. Something wasn't right here. Being released after what happened didn't make sense. Unless his interrogator already knew about his connection to Sterling. Unless he wanted to keep his interest secret.

That had to be the answer. Vince knew that Sterling was with Mac. Mac's plane had filed a return flight plan on arrival, and Sterling had boarded that plane. With the Secret Service and the FBI files available to Mr. Vincent Dawson, he'd already learned who Conner Preston was and probably why he was here. And he knew that Mac had Sterling.

Conner allowed himself a grim smile. He'd been surprised when Sterling had agreed to come to the wedding. Then he'd heard Mac would attend. Even then the connection hadn't come to him. It had been Erica who knew how often Sterling and Mac talked. She suggested the possibility that they might be intrigued with each other. Sterling had come a long way from the beaten-down young woman he'd met in the rehabilitation center of a hospital ten years earlier. But Sterling and Mac?

The more he thought about it, the more it made sense. Mac had lost his wife and Sterling had lost the use of her legs. Two wounded people who needed love. Not a bad idea.

Conner would leave Sterling in Mac's hands. He had a wedding to attend.

Then he'd do a little checking on Mr. Vincent Dawson.

THREE

A sense of peace enveloped Mac as the plane swept over the mountaintop where he'd built his sanctuary. It had been that way for a long time. The outside world brought pain; Shangri-la soothed it. The few trips he'd made away from New Mexico had been short unavoidable ones that grew less and less frequent as the years passed.

He glanced at Sterling and wondered what it was about her that had touched him so deeply. She couldn't be more than thirty-five, probably younger, and as much a recluse as he. With just her soft voice on the phone, she'd caught his fancy. Sterling, this stranger who never left Paradox, intrigued him.

Mac felt a connection with her that had eventually coaxed him away from his place of refuge. That bit of foolishness had thrown him into a complex situation. In previous times he'd been able to call on one of the people he'd helped before to return the favor by coming to the rescue of someone else. This time he was the one who was helping, because he was the person responsible for her plight.

What had he expected when he decided to attend the wedding? A safe, pleasant encounter with a woman whom he knew only through the phone? Or had he even let his imagination go that far? Whatever he'd anticipated, it hadn't been a dramatic flight from a murderer.

Sterling's eyes were closed, but the suggestion of a frown tugged at the corners of her mouth. Her chest rose and fell beneath the bulky ski sweater. There was a tenseness about the way she held herself. Yet, at the same time there was a gentle appeal that spoke to him. He wondered what she was thinking.

He wondered again why she'd come. He couldn't stop thinking about it.

Sterling could feel him watching her. She hadn't slept well last night. Excitement? Uncertainty? More than once, she'd decided to cancel her trip. If only she had.

Twice today she'd encountered a man who'd changed her life. The first one had tried to kill her. The second was trying to save her.

"It feels as if the plane is slowing down," she said, pushing herself up.

"It is. We're about to land. If you look, you'll see the sun setting beyond the mountain."

She turned toward the window. Mac's hard featured face was a silhouette against the vivid gold and purple of the sky. "It's beautiful," she whispered. "I can see why you love it here. Is your . . . is Shangri-la built on a mountain?"

Mac smiled. "Not exactly. It's built inside a mountain. Nobody can come in who isn't invited. You'll be safe there."

Sterling felt a clutch of emotion. He was wrong. Today had proved that. "There's no place you can be completely safe."

"I promise you'll be safe here, Sterling. Trust me."

She looked at him for a long moment. Trust him. Did she dare? What was she doing here with this man? Though few knew it, Conner had told her that Lincoln McAllister was one of the richest and most powerful men in the world. Why had he put himself in danger for her?

All the times they'd spoken on the phone, it had never been personal, mostly talk about the import-export business Conner ran. Sometimes about Conner's clandestine activities as "The Shadow," the special Green Beret name he'd earned because of his unique skills in undercover work.

Between the two of them, Mac and Conner helped people whose problems were special. If trouble came, trouble that couldn't be solved through normal channels, the world turned to Mac. And more often than not, he turned to Conner.

And she'd been the go-between. In the last year Mac had learned that she, too, was a night owl. And he'd called from time to time, a connection in the lonely hours of the night, a friend whose voice she'd come to know. They'd discussed books, music, art, philosophy, but never anything personal. She hadn't told him about her past, and she knew nothing of his.

"Trust you, Mac?" she repeated, compelled to answer honestly. "Yes, I think I do." Her fears suddenly seemed to subside. "If you live inside the mountain, then how do we get there?"

"We land on it. Then we take a special elevator down to the complex."

At that moment the plane dropped into a crater in which a landing field had been carved.

"Oh, Mac, it's like going through a tunnel with the sky as a ceiling. This must have cost a fortune." She swallowed hard and shook her head. "I'm sorry. I'm prying again. It's just that I'm so used to riding herd on Conner that I do it automatically, even when I know he makes enough money to afford anything he wants."

"So do I, Sterling. At least my family did. All I try to do is use the results of their labor in a way that does the most good for those who need help."

"What kind of business is your family in?"

"An easier question is what kind of business weren't they in? The truth is, Sterling, there is no *they*, not anymore. My father and two uncles were in business together. My father was the only one who married. He died when I was in college, and my uncles were killed in an explosion two years later. My mother was already gone. All the businesses have been sold now, except for the oil company that gave them their start and a research lab that I'm very involved in."

The plane slowed to a hover and circled a field cut out of towering peaks of granite. As it touched down and rolled to a stop, Sterling could see a steel door slide open and several people rush forward, one of them pushing a wheelchair.

Before she could stop Mac, he'd lifted her up out of the seat and started toward the door already being opened by one of his attendants.

"Put me down, Mac. I told you I *can* walk."

"I intend to," he said, clattering down the steps. "Hello, Raymond." He greeted the man with the chair and plopped Sterling into it. "Raymond's my assistant and security chief," he explained.

"Shall I take the lady to the guest quarters?"

"No. She'll be staying in the private wing. Mrs. Everett is preparing her room."

Mac brushed Raymond aside and pushed Sterling into the building and then into an elevator, pushing a button that closed the doors behind them.

"Mac, you don't have to make any special arrangements for me. I'll be perfectly happy to stay in your guest quarters."

"No," he said, a little too sharply, then forced a smile as he added, "until Conner and I decide what to do, you'll stay close to me."

"But—" She started to argue when the elevator stopped and the door slid open, revealing a deeply carpeted hallway lined with sconces and tables with mirrors and waist-high poinsettias. "It's Christmas," she said softly. "I'd forgotten."

"We don't have snow here, at least not unless some freak storm blows in. But our staff tends to be sentimental about everything even if I'm not. This is Angel Central, remember?"

The red-velvet-embossed wallpaper and dark green carpet was a perfect background for the white lights strung from sconce to sconce.

"Goodness, Mac. This is a castle."

"No, it's a fortress, Sterling. I built it to protect the people I . . . people who need love."

And he'd brought her into it. She didn't know what to say.

They reached an intersection that looked more like a family room. It was filled with softly filtered lights and a towering tree. Mac stopped beside it. It took Sterling a moment to realize that its ornaments moved from branch to branch. Someone on the staff had decorated the limbs with live red and green birds, whose singing filled the room.

"It's beautiful, Mac, a little unusual but beautiful. I've never seen another one like it."

"There isn't another one. The birds were all rescued from a rain forest that caught on fire. We couldn't save the trees but we managed to save these birds."

He pushed her chair past it, stopping at a door just beyond. He didn't have to knock; it opened immediately.

"Mr. McAllister," a woman said, standing back to allow them to enter the chamber.

"Mrs. Everett, this is Ms. Lindsey. She'll be with us for a while. Will you make her comfortable?"

"Of course, sir."

"Sir? Elizabeth, I've asked you over and over not to call me that."

"I know. But my mother would never have allowed me to be so informal. It isn't proper."

Mac turned to Sterling and shook his head. "Maybe you can help me take some of the starch out of her petticoat."

"But Mr. McAllister! I'm not wearing a . . ." Elizabeth's voice trailed off.

Mac gasped. "Elizabeth, you're not wearing a petticoat? What would your mother say?"

"I'm wearing a petticoat. It just isn't starched. Welcome, Miss Lindsey," Elizabeth said, laughing.

"You asked for a hot tub," Mac said, turning to face Sterling. "There's one in your bathroom. It has massage jets that will ease your muscles." He glanced at his watch. "I'll leave you for a rest. Please feel free to explore around the fortress if you get bored. There's a heated pool at the end of the corridor we crossed and a solarium created with artificial sunlight."

"Thank you," she managed, overcome by the elegance of the apartment he'd supplied. "I'm sure I'll be fine."

He started toward the door, stopped, and turned.

"Sterling, truly you don't have to worry. You'll be safe here."

She nodded.

He started forward once more, reached the doorway, then paused. "I don't suppose you'd . . . I mean, if you're not too exhausted, will you have dinner with me?"

She studied him, not understanding his hesitancy. Did he think she'd refuse his hospitality? Was he asking out of a sense of responsibility? He seemed—uncertain, a characteristic she'd bet he didn't display often.

"I'd be pleased to."

"Fine, about seven? I'll come for you."

She smiled and watched him leave.

"Miss Lindsey." The elderly woman who'd greeted them came forward. "I'm Elizabeth Everett. I've gathered some clothing for you. I wasn't certain of your size, but I think Mr. McAllister's guess was about right. Would you like to use the hot tub? Or perhaps you'd prefer a nap first?"

"*Mr. McAllister*'s guess?"

Elizabeth laughed. "All right, *Mac*'s guess. I only insist on formality to keep our relationship on a more businesslike basis. He tells me I should be friendlier but I don't think he's really all that comfortable with intimacy."

Sterling liked Elizabeth. She liked the idea that she called him Mac behind his back. That was at odds with her appearance. She was dressed in a smart black dress and pearls that said she was more than a lady's maid. And there was a smile of affection on her face. On closer examination, Sterling saw that her face was a bit misshapen and carefully made up.

"I really do work for Mr. McAllister, though I'm not exactly a housekeeper. I guess you could call me more of an old-maid aunt."

"I thought he said he had no family." *Except for Jessie, the woman he loves.*

"He—I'm not family. I came here years ago, after an accident that left my face badly burned. I was alone and reluctant to leave the mountain. At that time he needed someone, so he let me stay. It'll be nice having someone new."

"I appreciate your efforts, but I really don't need any help. I'm perfectly capable of taking care of myself."

"Oh, but Mac won't accept that. And neither will I. You may not need a maid, but perhaps you need a friend? Please?"

"All right," Sterling agreed. "But just when did he guess about my size?"

"He called from his plane and said we were to prepare these quarters, find you some clothing, and I'm to stay with you to see that you're kept . . . comfortable. We didn't know what to expect. This is the first time he's had a woman guest in the private section."

Sterling hardly heard Elizabeth's comments. As much as she liked the self-styled old-maid aunt, she cringed at the implication that she needed a keeper. "Stay with me? As in prisoner and warden? Thank you, Mrs. Everett, but I think I'd better have a little chat with Mr. McAllister." She stood and made her way awkwardly to the door, clasping the frame in an attempt to stand straighter. "Where will I find him?"

"Please, Miss Lindsey, don't do that. He'll think I offended you. It was my choice of words, not his."

Sterling heard the dismay in Elizabeth's voice and stopped. She was overreacting, a trait she'd developed along with her independence. Conner accused her of donning her independence like a coat of armor. Sterling Lindsey didn't need any help. She had her life under control.

But she didn't. Not anymore. That life was contained within a building back in Virginia Beach, and she was a long way from home.

"I'm sorry, Elizabeth. I guess I'm just tired. I think I'd like to try out that tub," she said, "if you'll help me."

The woman brightened instantly. "Good idea. I'll turn on the water and lay out your things."

Mac made his way to his private office. This room was the heart of Shangri-la, its mind and future direction. And it was all stored here, in his computer. With a few whirls and blinking lights he was into files where no "civilians" were allowed.

Being a law-abiding citizen was a given with Mac. It always had been. But he didn't have time to go through proper channels, and in this case, he wasn't sure that such an inquiry would be safe.

Mac glanced at his watch. He had only an hour. Damn! Why had he asked her to have dinner with him? He should have put her in the regular complex. She'd have private quarters there and she'd still be safe.

She just wouldn't be close.

Mac forced his attention back on his computer.

In a half hour he had a picture of the senator's aide. His name was Vincent Dawson, an orphan who had been extraordinarily successful. There was no record of any existing family members. Vincent came on the scene when he entered and worked his way through undergraduate school at the University of South Carolina. After that came law school at Georgia State University in Atlanta and finally a political role as a White House Fellow. From there he'd gone to work with Representative Abigail Gardner from Florida until she retired. There was a gap of a year before he reappeared as campaign manager for the then-governor of Louisiana's run for the Senate.

Vincent Dawson, aide to Senator March, potentially the next president of the United States. None of it made sense. Mac reviewed the period when Dawson was originally appointed to the congresswoman's staff. Those things didn't happen without a full investigation of the applicant. Interviews, transcripts, letters of recommendation. Abigail Gardner was a tough woman and smart. If she took Vince on, he had to have been even smarter and without any blemishes on his transcripts.

Mac couldn't say the same for March. His background had been shady, but he'd managed to build a strong power base and was a master at wheeling and dealing. The possibility of having him as president made Mac's skin crawl, but it could happen.

Ten years before Vincent Dawson had worn a black ski mask and robbed and killed a man for a million dollars in bearer bonds. That would have been about the time Abigail had retired. What had old Vince done in the year after Abby left Washington? What had happened to Abby? He went into some different files.

Then he found it, a newspaper headline proclaiming FORMER REPRESENTATIVE ABIGAIL GARDNER KILLED IN FIERY CRASH. AIDE ESCAPES WITH HIS LIFE. A few more inquiries revealed a family lawsuit over Abby's will naming Vincent Dawson heir to her estate. But this was one time Vince didn't win. The judge had declared Abby incompetent, and Vince had been stripped of his newfound wealth.

So, Vince lost his meal ticket. He would have had to go to work. How and where could he start over? What would a man do who had become accustomed to wealth and position and suddenly lacked both?

He'd steal a million dollars.

Mac relayed what he'd learned to Conner on a secure phone line. Conner's explanation that he was released because Vince knew where Sterling was made sense. That meant that in order to get to Sterling, Vincent had to breech the gates of Shangri-la, and to date, that had never been done.

When Mac impulsively invited Sterling to dinner, he hadn't thought about what that meant. Now, standing before his mirror, he studied himself. Dark trousers, white dinner jacket with a folded red handkerchief in the pocket, and shiny black shoes; he looked like a refugee from a forties movie.

It had been years since he'd worn the jacket. He was just about to remove it when there was a knock on the door, and Elizabeth appeared.

"Oh my, Mac, you look very nice."

"I look like an idiot," he protested.

"That's the same thing Miss Lindsey said. The two of you will match beautifully. Just you wait and see."

"I'm not sure this is a good idea, Elizabeth."

"I'm sure it is. I've set up your table on the balcony. Shall I bring her?"

"No. I'll get her. And, thank you, Elizabeth. You're excused for the evening. Unless—will she need you later?"

"Miss Lindsey is a very independent woman. Like you, she doesn't think she needs anyone. I'm not certain either one of you is right about that. Independence can become crippling."

Mac frowned. Elizabeth fancied herself his surrogate mother. Tonight she was certainly acting like one.

At Sterling's door, Mac hesitated, then knocked lightly. The door was only partially closed. It swung open to reveal Sterling standing by her window.

She looked around and for a moment felt dizzy. She'd complained that the dress Elizabeth had found was far too elegant for a simple meal. It clung to her body, emphasizing the round curves she'd developed as a result of being confined. There was a time when she'd been called long and lean. But that was no longer the case.

Now she wished that she'd followed through with the private trainer Conner had arranged, but the young man had referred over and over to the future relationships she would have once she got herself in shape. She hadn't wanted relationships. She'd had one and she'd learned that physical attributes were as important as mental equality. She had decided that physical appearances didn't matter to her anymore, and she allowed herself to develop the soft curves the dress was now showing off. Physical didn't matter. At least, it hadn't until tonight.

She forced herself to speak. "You're very handsome, Mr. McAllister. You look like Humphrey Bogart. Do you play the piano?"

"No, and neither did Bogie. Shall we go?"

He was doing it again, covering a moment of awkwardness with humour. What could she do but respond? "Of course. I haven't much experience in dining with rich handsome men. But I wouldn't miss this for the world."

"What about Conner?"

"Conner's married, so he doesn't count," she said, and waited for him to respond.

Instead, he simply pushed her chair forward, then held out his hand. She smiled and allowed him to assist her. "Where are we dining?"

"Where else? Mac's Place."

Red and green candles set in a nest of holly branches sent little curls of smoke into the night sky. A table for two had been placed beside a wall created by windows.

Sterling slipped into her seat, trying unsuccessfully to avoid any contact with Mac as he slid the chair forward. But he thwarted that by placing one hand on her shoulder. He leaned down, pointing at the night beyond the glass.

"Look at that view, Sterling. There's nothing like it anywhere else in the world."

A million glittering stars surrounded an icy white moon pinned on a black velvet sky like some elegant display in a museum. "Did you order this moon?" she asked, hearing the slight breathlessness she felt in her voice.

"No, I managed to create a complex that offers safe haven to the needy, and houses the most up-to-date medical equipment available to man. I have a staff that can solve almost any problem and the space and means to do it. Dozens of people scattered across the world take on trouble, from a mother who can't face the loss of a child to a patriot wishing to overthrow a cruel dictator. But creating something like this is beyond the capabilities of any of my earthbound angels."

"Do you really believe in angels?"

He straightened up and moved over to an entertainment center on the adjacent wall. "Sometimes," he said softly. "Sometimes there is no other answer."

A waiter appeared silently. He removed Sterling's napkin and gave it a shake before placing it in her lap. A bottle of wine was brought, opened, and tasted by Mac, who nodded and carefully watched as their glasses were filled.

Moments later piano music drifted into the air and added to the magic.

"Shall we make a toast?" Mac asked, lifting his glass.

Sterling held out her glass. "What shall we drink to?"

"To angels," he said, and tapped her glass, sending a lovely chiming sound that rippled around the room, as if the composer had written it into the evening's song. "And to forever after."

"Forever after?" she asked with a smile.

"Of course. This is Shangri-la, remember?"

She remembered. She also remembered something else he'd said. He'd said he was taking her to meet Jessie, the woman he loved.

FOUR

Mac had rescued Sterling, but he hadn't anticipated the effect it would have on him. Personally bringing her to Shangri-la had taken him back to a time before he'd built the complex, when he'd met another woman who had needed him. The first time he'd been the helping angel.

Long before he'd become Mac, he'd been Lincoln McAllister, playboy extraordinaire. He'd been on his way home from a party. He didn't remember who'd given it—life had been one party after another—only that particular night he'd had too much to drink and had insisted on driving himself home in his latest shiny black sports car.

Her name was Alice and she'd been standing at the side of the road, waiting for a car, any car. He'd seen her in the lights cast by the truck ahead. It slowed, then kept going. At first he'd thought she was about to cross the street. Then, as he'd reached the spot where she was standing, she had leaped into the path of his car.

Even now, late at night, he still heard the sound of screeching brakes and felt the thud as his fender caught her body and threw her into the air.

She hadn't died, not then. Her first attempt at suicide had failed. Six years later—after he'd married her and given her a child—the demons inside her head became more than she could handle, and she'd driven off the mountain, killing herself and critically injuring their little girl.

Now, as he watched Sterling across the table, he thought about what he was doing. He'd built a sanctuary for desperate people and he'd staffed it with professionals who could help. Slowly, over the last fourteen years, he'd expanded the scope of his enterprise. He'd had some success and with that came a kind of fragile, manufactured peace. All of his interventions hadn't been so dramatic. There were times when he'd simply read about someone somewhere who had a dream or needed one and he'd stepped in. But this was the first time he'd become personally involved with a woman who needed him since his wife Alice and their child. Why?

"Mac? What happens now?" Sterling's voice jerked him back to the present.

"Now? We have dessert, something sinfully delicious."

"No, Mac. No dessert. I'm not one of those eat-all-you-want, willowy people. Too many late-night dinners like this and I'll have to have an eighteen-wheeler to get around instead of a wheelchair."

"You're fine, Sterling. I lifted you, remember?"

She was fine. All through dinner he'd been reminded how fine. The dress Elizabeth had provided for her was made of a loose-fitting flimsy red material shot with a metallic thread that shimmered in the candlelight. She wore no jewelry, only a single strand of silver woven into the simple twist she'd fashioned at the back of her neck.

She was round, yes, but it was the kind of gentle softness that a man could cuddle up to and feel safe with. Simple, old-fashioned, and elegant.

"You're too concerned about your size," he added with a smile.

But she wasn't concerned, not really, just fluttery with the knowledge that he was interested in her. They were alone, in an intimate setting and they'd shared danger. That was intoxicating. But she thought that it was the situation, not the woman, that intrigued Lincoln McAllister.

She shook her head, consciously searching for a way to defuse the sexual tension. "Thank you, Mac, but I know what I am. The dinner was wonderful, but I think it's time we talk about what I'm doing here."

In one second she shattered the illusion he'd been building subconsciously throughout dinner. He wondered why he kept straying off into some sensual fantasy. He understood that's what it was. Fantasy, based on shared risk and loneliness. "Not yet," he said, too abruptly. "We get the facts, analyze them, and formulate our plan. By tomorrow we'll know more. Tonight we're simply two people having dinner."

Sterling laid her napkin down and studied him. "All right. But I am sorry you missed the wedding. I know how seldom you leave your mountaintop. I know you wanted to be there, since you and Montana are close friends."

"We are friends, but I would have been totally out of place at a wedding. Long ago I lost any talent I ever had for making small talk. The wedding was simply an—obligation. I helped Montana once when he needed help. Then he returned the favor by being one of Mac's Angels to help someone else."

"That's pretty cut-and-dried."

"That's what I am, Sterling. I joke about it, but I'm not a real angel. Don't give me that kind of credit. What I do is use what I have, to do what I . . . I can't do myself."

She didn't believe he was that cold. She'd seen the playful side of him, understood he used humor to cover up real emotion. "And me? Will I be asked to help someone else?"

"You will," he said solemnly. "You most certainly will."

She sat silent for a moment. "Well, the food was delicious and I appreciate you sharing Mac's Place with me. But I truly am very tired."

The strain in Sterling's voice made him feel

guilty. Having dinner with her had been pleasant. For a time she'd relaxed and forgotten the danger.

He had enjoyed the company.

Now she was fading. How long had he been staring at her without seeing? "I'm sorry, Sterling. Guess I'll have to admit it. I'm not really Bogart; I'm just an ordinary man."

She cocked her head to the side. "How's that? This place certainly isn't ordinary. What you've created here is unbelievable. In fact, I probably ought to be calling you James."

"Now, there you have me. James?"

"As in Bond. 007. You don't look like him, but if he doesn't have his American headquarters here, he ought to."

Mac grinned in spite of himself. She had a way of making him do that. She wasn't the first to make that comparison. It wasn't a personal comparison; it was more a matter of the lengths to which he went to succeed.

"Well, if I'm 007, who does that make you?"

"Why Moneypenny, of course. Secretary, assistant, and general nanny. That's a role I could probably handle."

"Perhaps," he said softly, remembering Sterling's voice on the phone. "Perhaps Moneypenny would tell me I'm falling behind in my duties." He stood, dropped his napkin, and pushed Sterling's wheelchair next to the chair she was sitting on. He held out his hand.

She took it and moved stiffly to her wheelchair.

"I think you've done fine so far, 007. What do you think you haven't done well?"

"Well, it has been a long day." He pushed her wheelchair into the corridor and back toward the wing where she was staying, adding, "I expect Bond would have thought about that. He would have taken you to bed an hour ago."

Sterling gasped.

"Damn! That didn't come out quite right. Maybe you'd better go back to calling me Barney instead of Bond."

"Not a chance. Barney could never have worn that tux."

Sterling's chair wheels made a whistling sound as they rolled down the silent corridor. She had said she was very tired. That was untrue. Her senses were awake and heavily charged by the closeness of Lincoln McAllister. Beginning with her dramatic airport rescue, they'd left Barney Rubble behind. Now they were playing out events that *could* have come straight from a Bond movie.

Shangri-la had to be big-screen imagination and action at its best, a secret hideaway designed to repair and protect. Then came a romantic dinner with a handsome man who'd worn a white dinner jacket and created a fantasy meant to distract and entice. Bond at his best. But that was where the comparison ended.

Mac was no ultrasophisticated ladies' man. The crook in his once broken nose and a scar on his cheek made Mac more real than any screen actor.

There was a sense of pain about him, pain buried so deep that he wouldn't share it easily.

Except maybe with Jessie. She had to remember Jessie.

To add to the swirling currents of danger and emotion, she'd been plopped down right in the middle of Christmas, a sentimental holiday.

Christmas was the one season Sterling avoided. Christmas was for children, for the mystery of promises made and kept. If there really were angels, they wouldn't tease her with the illusion of love and family and all that the season promised.

But they—Mac had done just that.

Low strains of Christmas music wafted down the corridor as if someone had just opened a door. "Hark the Herald Angels Sing . . ." Then it stopped as suddenly as it had begun.

"Did you hear that?" she asked.

"What?"

"Music?"

"No, but if you want music, or anything else, all you have to do is ask Elizabeth."

"Mac, I want to talk to you about Mrs. Everett. I appreciate your concern, but I insist that you release her from her duties as my companion. I can manage alone."

He reached her door and stopped, looking down at her. "She isn't assigned to you, Sterling. As a matter of fact, tonight she's attending a social function away from the family quarters."

"Good," Sterling replied, lacking the energy to

argue. "I wouldn't want to take up all her time. Except for mastering all your electronic gadgets, I can look after myself."

Even Sterling knew how slurred her speech sounded.

He studied her. She couldn't hide her exhaustion even though she tried. Mentally gritting her teeth, she stood and took a step forward, intent on proving that she could manage.

Under other conditions she might have, but tonight she stumbled, a groan escaping her lips. She'd sat for too long without moving. Now her legs were asleep and out of control and the pain sliced right through her.

Mac was beside her instantly, sliding his arm around her waist and supporting her faltering steps as she made her way to her bedroom.

"You may be right," she managed to say as she reached her bed. "Just let me sit down and I'll be fine."

"And you intend to sleep in your clothes? I don't think so. That dress, it's so clingy. It's bound to be uncomfortable, not to mention those—stockings."

"I can take care of myself," she repeated, and reached for the back zipper in her dress, thinking he would be forced to leave. The zipper caught in the fabric and refused to budge. Her hand dropped weakly back to her lap.

"Please, Sterling, let me?" He swung her around, reached up, and, before she could protest, caught the zipper at the back of her neck and gave it a jerk. The dress slipped down and puddled at her feet.

"Mac!"

"Don't panic, Sterling, I've seen women undressed before. I'm in the rescue business, remember?" He caught the half-slip and peeled it down, then lowered her to the bed and covered her with the robe lying at the edge of the mattress. "I'll get your nightgown."

From the time Sterling had looked into the eyes of the man who'd shot her, she'd felt as if she were in a bad dream. But never had her dreams—even the good ones—taken her to a bedroom in a mountain fortress where a man like Mac took off her clothing as if he did it every day.

She felt as if she were standing outside herself, watching, as he returned with a long-sleeved flannel garment.

"Well," Mac said, "I'll have to speak with Elizabeth. Betty Rubble might sleep in something like this, but not Moneypenny. I have it on good authority that 007's Moneypenny wears nothing at all."

"You do?"

"Of course," he said as he gently threaded the nightgown over her head. "Why do you think Bond is the perennial bachelor. He may play, but he always goes home, doesn't he? I think I'm going to have to update your wardrobe." Beneath the gown, he deftly unhooked her bra.

She managed to slide the bra off her shoulders, but her attempt to put her arms in the sleeves was an exercise in futility. At a time like this her spinal cord failed her, pinching off the muscles and nerves that controlled her movements. Mac watched for a moment, then took one arm at a time and inserted it into the proper sleeve.

"Shall I remove your stockings?" he asked.

"No! No, I'll . . . I'll do it." But when she leaned forward, her spine creaked a protest louder than her own choked-back moan.

"What you'll do, Sterling, is lie down." He removed her shoes and lifted her, placing her head on the pillow and her legs on the bed. He sat down beside her and reached for the hem of her gown.

"Please, Mac. Don't."

"Close your eyes, Sterling. Just this once don't try to be Superwoman. This is simply one individual caring for another. That's what I'll expect from you at some point. That's what angels do. Will you let me?"

She closed her eyes, trying desperately to breathe evenly so that Mac wouldn't know the wild desire that his touch caused her to feel. Since she'd been released from the hospital, the only man who'd touched her so intimately had been her therapist and that had lasted only as long as it took for her to find a woman to replace him.

Until she'd been shot, she'd considered her body physically desirable. That's what her fiancé had said, and she'd believed him. She'd lain in his arms after they'd made love and planned a future of togetherness. He really had tried to feel the same after her injury, but he hadn't. There came a time when he couldn't touch her anymore and they'd both known that whatever they'd shared was over.

Mac's fingertips moved lightly up her legs, to her hips, following the seam of her panty hose. He peeled them down, lifting one hip, then the other to remove the dark filmy hose. She tightened her muscles, trying to conceal the trembling that his touch set off.

What was happening here was wrong. Mac had deliberately not mentioned this Jessie he spoke of earlier, and she'd delayed asking about her. She couldn't justify this deliberate oversight, nor could she deny the strong desire to wrap her arms around this man, hold him close as he—

She swallowed hard. "Mac?" Her voice sounded shaky. She tried again. "Mac, thank you. I know you've gone out of your way to make me feel safe. But I think it's time for you to go."

He picked up her feet and completed his task of removing the hose, which he then rubbed between his thumb and forefinger. "These are very sheer. It must be like wearing moonlight."

"Moonlight?"

He laughed. "I know. I'm hopelessly romantic about some things. Sometimes, at night, when everything is quiet, I look out at the moonlight on the mountain peaks. It's like glass, shimmering, transparent.

"Sorry. Don't listen to me. I get punchy when

I've overdosed on the company of a beautiful woman. Good night, Sterling."

He leaned closer, pulled up the spread, and, as if he were tucking in a child, planted his lips on her forehead. "Sweet dreams."

Long after he'd gone she felt the heated circle his kiss had left and the echo of his words. *Moonlight.* This man definitely might be compared with Bond, but he wasn't Bond. He was a poet.

He was a lonely man.

A lonely man who loved a woman named Jessie.

Sterling didn't think she'd sleep, but she did. Deeply and restfully, without the nightmares she'd dreaded. When she woke the next morning, she was alone. But her clothes had been laid out for her, and there was a tray holding a silver coffee carafe and lovely English scones.

Gingerly, she sat up, uncertain about the after-effects of her flight from the senator's aide and the trauma of her evening with Mac. She didn't know which had been harder on her body. Both had pushed her to limits she'd avoided for ten years.

Not too bad. She flexed her knees and felt a stab of pain radiate down her leg from her hip to her ankle. At least she could feel it. Pain was more reassuring than the numbness that sometimes made it impossible for her to walk. She nibbled at a scone, then made her way into the bathroom and turned on the water in the shower. Leaving the flannel nightgown in a heap, she stepped inside, raising her face to the stinging pellets of hot water.

Five minutes later she stepped out and dried herself. She hoped that Mac had a big enough hot-water heater to fill the needs of his mountain occupants. She'd used more than her share.

Finally she dressed in a pair of rose-colored sweats and matching soft slippers, leaving her damp hair to dry untouched. It would turn into a mass of curls, but somehow that freedom appealed to her this morning. The only thing she missed was a window. The absence of it reminded her that she was inside a wall of rock, a prison that kept the bad guys outside. But it also kept the good guys inside.

A newspaper had been left on her tray. She unfolded it, searching for a reference to an incident at the New Orleans airport. There was none. Apparently the senator's arrival had been kept secret.

It was just like it had been before. If she didn't tell, she might die. If she told, nobody would believe her. Except Conner.

And Mac.

After she finished her coffee, she became restless. Maybe she shouldn't have been so adamant about looking after herself. Elizabeth would at least have been company.

"Where is everyone?" she called out. But no one answered.

She pushed her chair down the corridor toward where Mac had told her the pool and the man-made solarium were located. Just as she reached the end of the hall, the door opened and a slim figure wrapped in a beach towel dashed through, heading toward Sterling, colliding forcefully with her chair.

"Rats!"

It was a young woman, beautiful, tanned, and shapely in a skimpy suit. The girl slung her wet hair back and studied Sterling. "Who're you?"

"I'm Sterling Lindsey."

"You aren't supposed to be up here." She backed slowly away. "Do they know you've escaped?"

Sterling rolled her chair backward. She tried a smile. "Escaped? I suppose I did. But Mac—Mr. McAllister—gave me permission to explore."

She nodded. "Mac brought you *here*?" Strong disbelief stopped her flight.

"Are you okay?" Sterling asked, noticing her pale cheeks and colorless lips. The girl's breathing was fast and shallow, almost as if she were on the verge of a panic attack. She'd nearly frightened her to death. "You've been for a swim. I thought I might try out the pool a little later. Swimming is about the only exercise I can handle."

"The pool is through those doors. I'm the only one who uses it."

"Would you mind if I join you sometime?" Sterling asked.

She shook her head, but that wide-eyed look never changed.

"Shall I call Mac?" Sterling asked, beginning to worry.

"No! Don't do that. He'll just—I'm fine. Really,

I'm fine. I just have these panic attacks when I'm startled."

"I'm sorry. I didn't mean to frighten you. I was just looking for . . . company."

"That's okay," the girl said, trying to pull herself together. "I just didn't expect to see you. There's never anyone here. Who did you say you are?"

"Sterling. Sterling Lindsey. And your name is?"

She raised doe-brown eyes and attempted a wan smile. "My name's Jessie."

It was Sterling's turn to be speechless. This was Jessie, the woman Mac loved.

"All right, Conner," Mac said into the phone. "Here's what I know. Vincent Dawson checks out, at least on paper." He gave Conner the rundown about his undergraduate degree and law-school education.

"Then he went to Washington, latched onto the congresswoman and became—what? Her gigolo?" Conner asked.

"That's the assumption her children made when Abby died," Mac explained. "The judge ruled in favor of the children and took the estate away from Vince. Fortunately, the children got what was rightfully theirs."

Conner tapped his fingernails against the receiver. "So where does that leave us? Tell me what you want me to do. I've got to get back to Virginia and do something about replacing Sterling, at least temporarily. After that I'm yours."

Mac glanced at his watch, then out the window of his secluded office. Purposely, he'd left Sterling on her own this morning. She'd demanded privacy, assuring him that she could take care of herself. He figured it was time to let her find out how lonely a person could be in Shangri-la.

"I don't know yet, Conner. But don't tell Sterling she's being replaced. She'd be even more insistent that I take her home. What about setting up a computer here for her? We could tie it into yours and nobody would know she wasn't in the office."

"That could work," Conner agreed. "And it would leave a channel open for Vince to contact her."

"I'll get that set up right away. Call me when you get back to the office and we'll make the transfer."

"Back to Vince. What else have you found out?"

"I haven't checked it out yet, but I'm guessing that Washington didn't beg Vincent to stay when the congresswoman retired or to come back when she died. He had to get there another way."

"And?" Conner prompted.

"He joined Senator March's staff as a fundraiser. Our boy is charming and successful. When March got elected he rode his coattails back to the Capitol. Now he's a force to be reckoned with."

"So where does that leave us?"

"I'm not sure yet. For about a year after Abigail's death Vince disappeared. The rest all checks out. But there's something not quite right about all this."

"Well," Conner observed, "we know that he's a

killer and a thief. I'm a little hazy on my political history. Connect Mr. Dawson's rise to power with some dates. Would that missing year happen to be ten years ago?"

"Bingo!"

"So our boy's career goals suffered a sudden halt when he lost Abby's money. He had no job, no mansion, no fortune. What would that do to a man like Vince?"

"I'd say it would make him desperate." Mac frowned. "And desperate men do desperate things."

Conner nodded. "What do you want me to do?"

"First, tell me about the wedding."

"Very plantation—'Lawsy Miss Scarlett—Southern. Montana was beaming from ear to ear, and Katie was about the prettiest bride I ever saw."

"Outside of your Erica, you mean."

Conner's voice dropped. "You got that right. By the way, you missed our news."

"Oh? What news?"

"Looks like there'll be another little Shadow arriving in about eight months."

"That didn't take long." Mac felt a knot in the pit of his stomach.

"Are you there, Mac?"

"Congratulations, Conner. I'm happy for you. But that brings up another problem. This Vince is dangerous. He saw Sterling. By now, he knows where she is and he knows that she recognized him."

"So? He can't get to her there, can he?"

"No, but he'll find out that Sterling works for you. And that could put Erica at risk."

There was a long pause.

Conner finally spoke. "You don't think he'd—"

"At this point I don't know what to think. But we'd better be prepared. Why not bring Erica out here?"

"I'll try. But she's got her heart set on overseeing the new house we're building. I don't think she's gonna give that up. She's a woman with a mind of her own."

"Like Sterling," Mac said softly.

"I take it you believe Sterling's story about the murder. I hoped you would. She had a pretty rough time convincing the police that she wasn't somehow involved."

"Did you ever look into it, Conner?"

"Yes, I did. When I saw Sterling in that rehabilitation center, I just had to get into the investigation. But there were absolutely no leads then. And Sterling had been through too much to pursue anything. She just burrowed in and pulled the business around her like a shroud. Look after her, Mac."

"You be careful, too, Shadow. This could get a little messy."

"I will. By the way, Mac, about that quilting business you have going. Erica would like a pattern for a baby quilt."

"Quilting business?" Mac cringed. "How'd you find out about that?"

"The airport police interviewed that couple on

the plane. They thought it was a hoot, you running a quilting business from your home so the guys at the gym won't know what you're doing. That's while you're tending little Conner—thanks, Dad—and Rhett and Erica. Next time make up a better story."

"Stuff it, Conner," Mac growled. "Besides, I had help. Sterling came up with the quilting business."

Conner laughed. "Very creative, our Sterling." He grew serious. "Just one final question?"

Mac sighed. "What?"

"Is your new baby really going to be a girl?"

The sound of Mac hanging up the phone bounced off the walls of his office like a stray bullet.

After he'd sat awhile, Mac allowed himself a smile. New baby? He was older now, calmer. Still, the idea of a new baby was absurd, even if it was imaginary. He'd promised himself a long time ago that he'd never allow himself to care about another woman again, because he couldn't trust himself to protect her or that love. Even though he'd tried, look what he'd done to Jessie.

Time to get back to work. Time to find out who Vince Dawson really was and, more important, what his next move would be.

FIVE

Sterling pushed open the door at the end of the hall and gasped. She'd never in her life seen anything like Jessie's swimming hole. She felt like she'd journeyed straight into a rain forest.

The indoor pool was fed by a natural waterfall that cascaded down into a deep rock-lined pool below. Mac's special illumination created the illusion of real sunlight, making the trees and flowering plants around the room look like the natural beauties of a tropical paradise.

Colorful birds, chirping a language of their own, sat perched in the branches. And the flowers; orchids, lilies, hibiscus, and gardenias grew in profusion, their perfumes sweetly scenting the air. It would have been too potent if not for the fresh gentle breeze that ruffled the branches and kept the odors from overwhelming the senses.

Sterling parked her chair at the end of the pool

and watched the water disappear into the rocks. What a peaceful place to unwind. She could see little tendrils of heat rising from the water. A hot springs here in the middle of a mountain. A place where an injured body could soak up sun, be rejuvenated, and feel safe at the same time.

Was all this for Jessie? Why? A girl as beautiful as she was ought to be on a real beach—with moonlight and a handsome lover lying beside her, not enclosed here in an artificial world. Something was wrong.

"I see you found the pool," Mac said.

With the chirping of the birds and the musical sound of the water, she hadn't heard him come in. She still didn't see him, but her senses told her he was standing just behind her chair.

"Yes. I don't know how you did it, but it's very beautiful. I can't believe we're inside a mountain."

"Believe it. The men who hauled in all the rock thought I was nuts. But they weren't as skeptical as the engineer who had to build a generator large enough to heat and light the entire complex."

"How long did it take you?"

"Oh, I'm still working on it. This wing was built first. It's been here for almost fifteen years. The other wings and floors evolved from there. I keep a full-time construction and maintenance staff on hand."

"They must not have families."

Mac suddenly moved to where she could see

him. He sat down on one of the rocks near her. "But they do. What makes you think they wouldn't?"

"I don't know. I guess I see Shangri-la as something like a space station, isolated . . . restricted. A place where you'd spend six months on duty and six months on R and R."

Mac looked surprised. "All the people who work here have the option of bringing their families. There is a grocery store, a small department store, restaurants, a movie house, and a recreation center. If we don't have it, it can be ordered in."

"But they're living underground."

"Do you feel like you're living underground here?"

Sterling glanced around. "No, I don't."

"You just want to be able to go outside. Is that it?"

She nodded.

"I'm told that back in Virginia you have an office on the beach. How often do you go outside, Sterling?"

She paused.

"Almost never, but I can see the outside world."

"So can the residents. The rooms that don't have windows, and that's most of them—for safety reasons—have holographic images on at least one wall. Your room has the same ability as the others. If you want to be on the beach, you just program your computer. Didn't Elizabeth show you?"

"No. I mean she probably would have, but I felt

uncomfortable having her there. I asked her to leave."

"Are you always so independent?" Mac challenged.

"I am. Are you always so controlling?"

He laughed. "Are we about to have our first fight?"

"I don't fight."

"All right. I have something to show you."

"Something more spectacular than this?"

"You may think so. Will you allow me to push your chair?"

"Do I have a choice?"

"Tsk, tsk, Moneypenney. What would 007 do with a testy secretary?"

"He'd probably have some kind of secret weapon that he'd use to convince her to take orders."

"Oh?" He leaned down and whispered in her ear. "You think he'd charm her into obedience?"

Sterling couldn't quite field a comeback to that. As they threaded their way down a path between the trees, she tried desperately to recall the Bond movies she'd seen. All she could remember was Pierce Brosnan brushing up on his Danish in bed with a buxom blonde.

"I don't speak Danish," she said suddenly, rather proud of herself for coming up with a line that caused Mac to falter in his pushing.

After a moment he replied seriously, "I'll teach you."

They reached an archway in which opaque sliding doors silently opened.

"No 'shazam'?" she asked.

"Picture ID," he explained.

"What about me?"

"Your picture has already been fed into the computer identification system."

Walking through the hallway, Sterling noticed that the decor changed dramatically. No more champagne wallpaper. Only utilitarian walls and tiled floors filled this space.

"Where are we going?" Sterling finally asked, beginning to feel uneasy.

"We're going to my office."

"Why?"

They approached a steel door, which automatically slid open. Once more they walked into another world. Silent, luxurious, but somehow Spartan at the same time. A wheat-colored couch hugged one wall. Along another lay a bank of computer screens and electronic equipment. A ratty-looking desk chair seemed to crouch between the computers and a large mahogany desk. But the most amazing feature of the room was a jagged outcropping of rock surrounding a shiny panel of wallpaper.

"Now watch this, Moneypenny."

He keyed a code into a panel on the wall. The panel slid open. A blue sky full of sunshine filled the opening.

"Holograph?" she whispered. "Amazing."

"No, this view is real." He rolled the chair forward. "There are times when I have to see the outside world."

"But you do it from a distance, don't you, Mac?"

"Yes. I find it's safer that way."

"And Jessie? Tell me about her, Mac."

He cut a sharp gaze toward her. "You met Jessie?"

"She was coming from the pool. I nearly scared her to death. Don't you ever have company?"

"Did she . . . what did she do?"

"She seemed surprised that I was there. I believe she thought I'd strayed from wherever your outside guests are housed." Questions about Jessie whirled through her mind. Sterling had to remind herself that she, too, was a quest. "Do you really think keeping her isolated is good for her?"

Mac walked past her and stood at the window looking out. This morning he was dressed as informally as she. He wore scruffy running shoes and sweats, as though he'd just come from a workout. A towel was draped around his neck, and his hair was still wet.

"I don't keep her here against her will. I've done everything I can to get her out, but she simply refuses to go. She doesn't want to leave ever."

"Mac, she's too young to know what she wants. I think she's probably very lonely here."

He swung around, clasping the ends of his towel. "You're right. She *is* lonely. And she ought to have outside friends."

"She must love you very much, Mac. That's why she stays."

"Yes, she loves me. In spite of the fact that I'm responsible for the death of her mother, she loves me."

Sterling felt as if a large object had just fallen out of the sky and landed on her. Had she misinterpreted something? "You killed her mother?"

"In a manner of speaking. I was gone when Jessie was born and most of the time when she was growing up. Still playing the rich man's son when I should have been at home. I knew she was fragile, that she fought a losing battle with depression but I refused to change my life. I hold myself responsible for what happened to my wife and to my daughter, Jessie."

"Jessie is your daughter?"

"Of course. Did Jessie tell you?"

"No. I think I scared her to death. She was on the verge of complete panic."

"Yes. She panics easily. Emotionally, Jessie is still a child. Her doctors have told me that maybe I've been too ready to go along with her fear of outsiders."

Sterling must have managed to nod enough to convince Mac she was listening but all she could think about was that he'd said he was taking her home to meet the woman he loved and that woman was Jessie. His beautiful daughter.

Last night at dinner, Mac had been playful and teasing. Afterward, when he'd undressed her, she'd felt such an unexpected awareness of him as a man. Guilt had assaulted her afterward. Guilt because she'd been attracted to a man who was committed to someone else. Even more upsetting was that she'd sensed that he'd been attracted to her too.

"Mac, before I met the real Jessie, I thought she was your lover."

"And you were jealous?" He lifted his chin and closed his eyes, then grinned as he moved close to her. "Give me your hand, Sterling."

"Why?"

"Because I'm asking you to."

She wasn't ready for her response, for her traitorous body to cause her to lift her hand independent of her command and rest it in his.

"Now stand."

"I'd rather not. Yesterday was pretty exhausting. I try not to overexert myself." What she couldn't say was that she wasn't certain her legs would hold her up. He was too close. With the sunlight behind him, his dark eyes were shaded and veiled.

"Stand up, Sterling," he repeated, then added, "please?"

He wasn't going to allow her to refuse his—request.

"I have to put up the footrests," she said, her voice tight, trying not to show the nervousness coursing through her body.

"Let me." He knelt, twisted the metal plates to the side, and placed her feet on the floor. "Now." He held out his hand again.

"No, I stand alone," she said. Taking a deep breath, she slipped toward the front of the chair, placed both hands on the armrests, and pushed herself up.

As she stood, her breasts grazed his body. He hadn't stepped back as she'd expected. Now they were touching, just enough to send an unwelcome ripple of response down her spine, which sometimes refused to register sensation at all.

She looked up at him. "Now what?"

"Now? This." He kissed her, a low groan accompanying the pressure of his lips. She resisted for a second, then felt her own lips part. The kiss changed, his mouth nipped at hers lightly, then recaptured hers with restrained desire. There was no mistaking his control, until she moved against him and felt his body throbbing as she swayed.

His body was firm. His arms as tight as steel bands. No escape was possible, and for just a moment she allowed herself to give in and be the desirable woman she had once been.

She knew he hadn't brought her to his office to ravish her. Why would he? Conner called her a "dish," but Conner always teased her. Sure, some of the men with whom he'd had business had sent out feelers, but she'd turned them all away. She'd been in love once, truly in love. And when her fiancé rejected her, she knew there was no such thing as forever. And she had no intention of taking any chances with her hard-earned peace of mind.

Jerking away, she pushed Mac back and dropped

into her chair. "Why did you do that?" she asked, cursing her breathlessness.

He frowned slightly as if he were considering his answer. "Surely you know. I wanted to kiss you last night, but I didn't want to take advantage of you."

This time she was the one confused. "But why didn't you kiss me last night?"

"Because I'm supposed to be protecting you, and right now you're vulnerable. Besides, I couldn't let you know that you scare the hell out of me."

She could only look at him in amazement. "I scare you?"

"Oh, lady. You do. And if you don't want me to kiss you again, we'd better get out of here and into your office."

"My office?" Like some kind of echo, she kept repeating his words. "You're taking me home?"

"For the time being, you *are* home. Conner and I talked. We decided that you'd be happier if you were busy, so we connected your computer at Paradox, Inc. with a computer at Angel Central. All your calls will be relayed here and nobody will be the wiser."

"I didn't know you could do something like that."

"And we're banking on nobody else knowing that we can."

"Surely you don't plan to keep me here forever, Mac. I have a life of my own."

"Sure you do. Just like me and Jessie even though it is one closed up in a building. There's just one difference. So far as I know, nobody is trying to kill us."

"I've set up your office close to me," Mac said, indicating a small room adjacent to his own office. He rolled her inside. From the dents in the linoleum it was obvious that some kind of heavy equipment had recently been removed. Now there was only a desk, computer, printer, and telephone, placed in front of a rock-framed window similar to the one in Mac's office.

"I have the wall open so you can enjoy the view," he explained, trying deliberately to smooth the transition between the fire of their kiss and the more routine mood of an office. "A touch of the button on your desk closes the wall, if need be."

"Why would I need to close it?"

"You probably never will, but the designer felt that for security purposes, the special panes might not be completely shatterproof."

"What, is an eagle going to crash through?"

It was obvious that Sterling was also trying to reinstate a business relationship. From the deep breaths she was taking, Mac wasn't certain she was having any better luck than he. "Remember the kind of work I'm in. Sometimes I deal with international situations. International figures who have enemies. There are other 'birds' that might be a danger— helicopters, for example."

"Mac, I appreciate what you're trying to do for

me, but I really don't think this is necessary. I'm sure that Conner can set up enough security in our office. And I'd really be more comfortable in my own apartment."

Mac rolled her to her desk and propped himself on the edge of it. "Sterling, you have to understand how serious this is. I didn't want to tell you this and frighten you, but your apartment was ransacked last night. We can't take any chances with a guy like Dawson. He is too dangerous."

"Mr. Dawson? Is that his name?"

"That's the name he's using, Vincent Dawson, former aide and personal assistant to Abigail Gardner, a congresswoman from Florida. Now he's latched onto Senator March."

She took another quick deep breath and held it.

"You said the name he's *using*. Do you think that really isn't his name?"

"We don't know. We're working on it. For now, the name of the man who killed your employer and shot you is Vince Dawson."

Her fear had a name. Somehow that made it more real. And that fear had invaded her apartment in Virginia, destroying the safety she'd built there.

"What about the office? Was it . . . broken into also?"

"It might have been except for the armed guards Conner had surveilling it. He pulled them out this morning. By now, there's nothing there. All the records have been transferred here."

"And Conner? And," she added with alarm, "what about Erica? Won't this put her in danger?"

"Not to worry. She's been sent to stay with friends in Germany. Conner had her flown out of the country by a private plane. We don't think Mr. Dawson will be able to find out where she is."

"I'm glad. Conner is a fool about her and now she's expecting a baby."

"He told me. Hard to believe he's that excited about a child."

Sterling thought about that. "Not really. Conner's been pretty lonely for the last few years. He wants a family."

"And you're a part of that family, Sterling, and always will be."

"Oh, Mac. I'm so sorry. I thought all this was over. If I hadn't decided to go to the wedding . . ."

He couldn't stop himself. He reached down and tilted her chin up with one finger. "You wouldn't have come to the wedding if it hadn't been for me, would you?"

Wide-eyed, she shook her head. "And you wouldn't have come, except for me, would you?"

"No. So now I have to protect you long enough for us to figure out what all this means. Couldn't we agree to a truce, just for a while?"

"I wasn't aware that we were at war."

"Oh, we're in the middle of a minefield, all right, Sterling. Don't you hear the bombs exploding around us? I just can't decide if we're at war with each other or with our own selves."

"Mac, I don't know if I can do this," she said in a low, strained voice.

"I can understand that. I'm having a little trouble myself."

"Am I responsible for that?"

"You are."

"I'm sorry, Mac. I know I'm not the only person here who needs your help. Please don't let me interfere with your angel work."

"Don't let you what? I've spent fifteen years not letting anything or anyone interfere with my angel work—until now. There comes a time, apparently, when the head angel, wherever or whoever he is, makes an executive decision that erases anything he doesn't agree with."

"You sound angry."

"I am—disturbed. Right now I don't need to be aware of the texture of your hair, the smell of your skin, the way you shiver just a little when I touch you. Kissing you is something I don't need. Wanting to slip into your bed and lie naked against you is definitely not conducive to conducting business rationally. But that's what I want."

The picture Mac created jumbled the words in Sterling's mind. Lying next to him, bare skin against bare skin, feeling her nerve endings shiver. Oh yes, she understood.

She understood that they were saying no but their desire was taking over and reaching out for each other. She had to stop this before it would be too late.

"I'm not very experienced with men and casual relationships, Mac. I never expected to have this kind of response to a man. I . . . I thought my sexual responses were dead."

"Sterling, there's nothing casual about this relationship. Your sexual drive isn't dead, it's just been asleep. You were content with that. But Vince changed everything for both of us. Now we've got to figure out what to do about it."

"You figure it out," she said suddenly, moving her chair back through the doorway into Mac's office and to the exit door that opened instantly. "I'm going . . ." Where was she going? "I'm going to take a swim."

"The pool is heated, Sterling. And I think you're hot enough already."

"Then I'll take a cold shower."

He followed her to the door. "Sterling, if it's any consolation to you, I promise I won't put pressure on you."

She didn't answer. He didn't have to put pressure on her. She was doing a good enough job of that herself. She already admired and respected Mac. She'd become his friend long before this. She was in big trouble. She needed to go back to her room and think.

She met Elizabeth there carrying an armload of books and tapes. "I was just leaving these for you," she said. "I'll be out of your way in just a moment."

"What are those?" Sterling asked.

Elizabeth smiled and held out one of the tapes.

Danish Made Easy. "I think it's wonderful that you want to learn a language while you're with us. And I'm on my way to the shop to find new—sleeping attire. Personally, I think your flannel nightgowns are quaint."

"Thank you, Mrs. Everett. Just leave the tapes. But you don't have to shop for any nightgowns. I like the flannel one just fine."

She thought she heard Mrs. Everett laugh, then decided she was just delusional. Until she rolled herself into the bedroom and discovered the hologram that covered the wall opposite her bed.

There was a life-size scene of 007 and a blonde in a bed.

The blonde wasn't wearing any clothes.

SIX

"What did Sterling say when you told her we were transferring the Paradox records to Shangri-la?" Conner asked.

Mac picked up the handset and turned off his Speakerphone. Discussing Sterling, even in the ultimate safety of his own office, was too public. "She said she wanted to go home, that you'd protect her. Conner, I had to tell her about her apartment."

"Damn! That must have wiped her out. That apartment and the office have been her only safe havens. Now she's lost both."

"Conner, I think we're going to have to call in a few high-level IOUs. Who can we trust?"

"I've been thinking about that. I have a friend who's a retired Army general. He's an adviser to some committee so secret that it doesn't have a name. And there's an investigative reporter with the *Post*. What do you have in mind?"

"Well, I've been in touch with a securities expert who can be trusted. And an ex-FBI agent with friends. I say we call a meeting of minds. Think we can fly them to New Mexico, without the world knowing?"

Mac thought about it for a minute. "Considering that it's Christmas, I'm not sure we can pull these men away from their families. What about a teleconference on a secure line?"

The ex–Green Beret looked at his watch. "It would take a couple of days to set it up. It's only ten days until Christmas and they're scattered everywhere."

"Get me names and numbers. Let's try for three days from now."

"Fine," Conner answered. "I'd like to wrap this up in time to join Erica for a little celebrating of our own. This will be our last Christmas alone. After that, it'll be Santa Claus and the whole family bit."

Mac thought wistfully about Sterling and his made-up story of spending Christmas in Aspen with their imaginary children. There'd been very little real celebrating at Christmas since Jessie had gotten too old for Santa. He didn't know how long it had been since either of them had gone to the little chapel on the lake at the base of the mountain. At some point they'd stopped trying to live a normal life.

"Get the names and numbers. I'll make it happen," he said, and broke the connection. The mythical home in Aspen, the fictitious twins and baby,

Sterling's fake pregnancy—all swirled around in his head.

Christmas, children, and family was so appealing to Mac. He wondered if Barney ever had the kind of lascivious thoughts about Betty that Mac was having about Sterling? From what he remembered about Betty, Barney had probably done something right. Betty married him.

Mac might be able to put Sterling's office duties off for a day or two, but sooner or later she'd be working in the room next to him. That was too close. He should have put her in the basement.

Instead of thinking about Barney and Betty, he'd send for all the Bond videos and study up on how to be suave, debonair, and sexy. It had been a long time since he'd even tried.

No. For now, he had to get his mind on the problem at hand. He had to figure out how to set a trap for a murderer.

Sterling would have deleted the hologram of Bond and the blonde sex kitten, if she could have figured out how the control panel worked. Elizabeth would be able to do it, but she'd dismissed the kindly woman again. She just couldn't escape the devilish expression in Bond's eyes.

Eyes just like Mac's. She didn't know why she hadn't noticed that similarity before. Their appearances were so different, she'd missed it. Even so, she'd certainly noticed everything else about Mac. And what she hadn't seen, she'd imagined.

Here she was, inside a mountain, with no way to get out. No way to reclaim the life she'd so carefully built for herself since leaving the rehabilitation hospital. Why had she left Virginia?

Because of Mac. She'd been intrigued, stimulated in a way she'd never thought possible. Especially, not after the accident. And she'd fooled herself into thinking that she could function in the real world without being haunted by the memory of her attacker.

Well, she couldn't. She might as well resign herself to a life of contented restrictions, a comfortable life that gave her everything she could possibly want. Conner had a place in Germany, high in the mountains, where she could go when she wanted a change of scenery. He had a private plane to fly her there and a staff to see to her comforts. She had more money than she'd ever need, anything she wanted in the way of possessions, friends—a limited number of them, but there when she needed them. That was all she required and more than most people ever had.

Why was she, a grown woman at the age of thirty-two, feeling such physical reactions to this *man*? A man was something she could do without. She'd been there, done that, with disastrous results. If she could walk, she'd be pacing the floor. Instead, she was simply flexing and unflexing her fingers around the arms of her wheelchair.

"Damn you, Vincent Dawson! You had no right to steal my life!"

There was a knock on her door, timid, but insistent.

"Come in," she called out, and turned to face the intruder.

The door opened slowly.

"Well, come in. If it's you, Mac, we have to have a little talk about the hologram on my wall."

The door opened fully to reveal Jessie standing hesitantly in the corridor. "It's me—Jessie."

She was dressed in jeans and a University of New Mexico sweatshirt, her hair pulled back in a limp ponytail.

"Great," Sterling said. "I'd love to have some company who isn't inclined to give me orders."

Jessie laughed, revealing what Sterling guessed was a rare glimpse of the real Jessie, not the timid and scared girl she met outside near the pool.

"I thought I was the only one who got treated like a child by my father," Jessie said, leaning against the door as if she were ready to flee at a moment's notice, if necessary.

"No way. It seems to me that children, old people, and handicaps all get the same treatment: rules, restrictions, orders, lies, and platitudes. Do come in. I promise I won't give you any of them."

Jessie nodded, raising her gaze and fixing it on the wall behind Sterling. "Wow! They wouldn't let me have that on *my* wall. How'd you do it?"

Sterling blushed. "It's your father's idea of a joke."

Jessie eyed her skeptically. "Joke? Mac doesn't joke—ever."

"Sure he does," Sterling continued. "He's very quick with his comebacks and he has an interesting imagination when he needs it."

Jessie laughed out loud. "Mac? You sure we're talking about the same man?"

"I find your father to be a very complex man, Jessie."

"How so? He's always seemed pretty much a drill sergeant with an angel complex to me."

"Think about it. He looks like a boxer, has the dictatorial habits of a marine sergeant. At the same time he's sly, underhanded, manipulative, and as charming as . . . as James Bond."

Jessie took a long look at Sterling, then smiled. "You could have fooled me." She glanced at the hologram again. "Then again, I'm just his daughter. I wouldn't know about his other charms."

Sterling closed her eyes. Jessie seemed inclined to be friendly, but she was getting into hot water here. "Jessie, could you turn that thing off. No, show me and I'll do it."

"Sure." The girl moved to a panel beside the door and turned, waiting for Sterling. "I don't think you can reach it."

Sterling brought the chair beside Jessie and locked the wheels. She pushed herself up, ignoring the tingle of pain that shot up her spine. "I can stand, Jessie. I just don't do a lot of walking. It's not that I can't; it's just very painful for me."

"Is that why Mac brought you here? So that our doctors can work with you? They really do great things. They made me walk again." She sounded relieved.

"The panel, Jessie. Let's get that done first."

"Oops! Sorry. This button turns it off and closes the window. If you want to choose another view, hit this button and it brings up a menu of choices. There are beaches, mountains, farms, cities, anything you want, so long as it doesn't have to be real."

Sterling hit the close button, then sat down. "I'm hungry, Jessie. Could we have lunch together and you tell me more about—how the doctors taught you to walk?"

She grinned. "I'd rather talk about my father."

"Food first," Sterling insisted.

"Okay. Want to eat here or . . . how about the Hard Rock Café?"

"You have a Hard Rock Café? No, don't answer that. Just tell me how loud the music is."

"We can have it loud, or we can turn it down. Haven't you figured it out yet. This place makes Michael Jackson's Neverland look like a cheap road show. We can have anything that money can buy."

"Just so long as James Bond isn't there, I'm ready."

The Hard Rock Café turned out to be another hologram in the recreation room. Jessie pushed

Sterling's chair into the small eating area complete with sports equipment and a jukebox.

Jessie handed Sterling a menu. "What would you like?"

Sterling studied the selection and decided on a HRC hamburger. Jessie nodded, picked up the phone, and ordered two burgers and extra french fries.

"Have you ever eaten at the real thing?" she asked, a tinge of excitement in her voice.

"No, have you?"

"Naw. But Burt, the chef, has and he duplicates anything they serve."

Sterling studied Jessie. She might be twenty. But devoid of makeup and covered with a loose sweatshirt, she looked younger. "Wouldn't the real thing be more fun?"

"No." Her reply was a keep-off sign as big as a skyscraper. "I don't leave the mountain."

But Sterling never backed down, not when she was trying to help make someone else's life better. "Why?"

"I . . . I just don't. Why are you in that wheelchair?"

"Because I was in an accident—no, that's not true. I must be honest with you. I was shot."

"How? Was it your husband? Didn't you two get along?"

"You must watch too many soap operas here Jessie. No, it wasn't my husband. I was never married.

The man who shot me also robbed and killed the man I worked for. I just got in the way."

"Wow! And Mac brought you here to learn to walk?"

"No, Mac brought me here to protect me."

Jessie looked confused. Sterling knew she'd started the painful story, and now she would have to finish it. But that confession would demand that Jessie share her history as well. "If I tell you all my secrets, you have to tell me yours. Deal?"

Reluctantly, Jessie agreed. "I guess so."

Sterling explained that she'd been late leaving the copy room, walked in on the killer as he was emptying the safe, and was shot. She'd fallen, hit her head, and lapsed into a coma that left her with a sketchy memory for months. "The medical staff determined that the bullet was too close to the spine to risk surgery and left it there. That was ten years ago."

"You mean you've been walking around with a bullet still inside you ever since?"

"Yes, and it happened to lodge itself near my spine and interfere with my walking. I'm not really steady and it's quite painful."

"But Mac's doctors can fix it. They can do almost anything."

"I'm sure they can. But that's not why I'm here."

"I don't understand. What is Mac protecting you from?"

"The man who shot me got away. Nobody ever knew where he was until yesterday. I saw him and he saw me. Mac and Mr. Preston brought me here so that he can't find me and harm me again."

"Weren't you scared?"

"I was scared. I'm still scared. But that's enough of my story. It's your turn. Why couldn't you walk?"

"My mother and I were in an automobile accident. Both my legs were broken. She was killed."

"Oh, Jessie. I'm so sorry. That must have been awful. How old were you?"

"About five, I think. It seems so long ago. I don't remember much about it."

"I know how that is. You just block out the pain, don't you?"

"You too?" She looked up anxiously.

"Sure. You don't think you're the only one to close off everyone and everything, do you?"

"I guess I never thought about anyone else. There's always been just me—since the accident."

"But you walk fine now, don't you?"

"Yes."

Sterling looked around to see if anyone was listening, then asked, "Why don't you get out of this place and find a real Hard Rock Café?"

But she'd have to wait for Jessie's answer. The chef, a heavy, round-faced man who obviously sampled his wares, brought in their food.

"Hard Rock Special burger for you, Jessie, and another one for Ms. Lindsey, just like you ordered. Ms. Lindsey, are you sure you wouldn't rather have something else?"

"Nope. When in Rome, do as the Romans, or in this case the rock stars."

"If you need anything, just ring," he said as he left. "And turn up the rock-and-roll music, Jessie. If you're going to give Ms. Lindsey the food, she might as well have the atmosphere."

"Do you want it turned up, Ms. Lindsey?"

"Please, no. The food and the decor is enough. I want to hear some answers."

"What do you want to know?"

"Why you never leave this mountain? Don't you go to college?"

"Oh, yes. I'm a sophomore. I have my own private tutors."

"Which college lets you stay at home with a private tutor?"

"The one where Mac built a new wing. I'm not the only one there. Sometimes there are others, people who can't go to regular classes."

"Of course. If you have enough money, you can have anything. You told me. But don't you miss having friends?"

"I have friends. The people who work here have kids. Of course, they're mostly younger, but some of the workers and I watch movies in the rec room. We play billiards. Sometimes they come to my pool."

"But what about my original question? Why don't you just walk right out of here?"

"I—I can't."

Sterling looked up. "You mean Mac won't let you?"

"Mac lets me. Or he would."

Sterling continued, "You don't look sick. You're not in a wheelchair. You could live on campus. Why don't you?"

"You don't understand. I just . . . can't."

Jessie's hands started to shake. Her face went chalk white and her breathing became labored.

"Jessie, it's all right. I won't force you to tell me if you'd rather not talk about it." Sterling laid her hand on the girl's arm. "Breathe slowly. In and out. In and out."

The hyperventilating slowed and color started to return to Jessie's face.

"Just remember, Jessie, I've been in some bad places in my life, so I understand your troubles. And, as one recluse to another, I'm here if you want to talk about it. Now finish that burger and tell me what the chef's favorite dessert is."

"How'd you know he likes dessert?"

Sterling gave her young friend an amused look. "You must be kidding. I just saw him, remember?"

As quickly as Jessie's fearful mood had come, it disappeared. "Well, I hate to disappoint you, but Burt loves everything. He can even make yucky things good. Mac won't let me in the kitchen anymore. He says that I'll end up looking like Burt, and he'll have to roll me around."

"Mac—why do you call your father 'Mac'?"

"I don't know. I guess I just copied other people. When I was little, I never heard anyone say 'father,' or 'daddy' or even 'dad.' I never thought about it before."

Sterling wiped her mouth with her napkin and laid it on the table. "Okay, enough bad stuff. Let's talk about something fun. What are you getting for Christmas?"

Jessie went blank. "For Christmas? I don't know. Usually, all I do is ask for something and Mac gets it. There's nothing special I want."

"You haven't written a letter to Santa?"

Jessie grimaced. "Sterling, Santa doesn't come to see me. I'm twenty years old. I haven't believed in Santa Claus since I was eight."

"Well, no wonder he doesn't come. Didn't anyone ever tell you that so long as you believe, he continues to show up?"

"No. Who told you a dumb thing like that?"

"My—no, not my mother. My mother told me that Santa Claus was a rich old man with a bag full of money. She kept believing that until she found a real man who fit the description."

"What happened then?"

"She put me in a boarding school and left the country."

"That's awful. How old were you?"

"I was twelve."

"But she came back for you, didn't she?"

"No. Her husband eventually found someone younger and left my mother. He gave her enough money to buy her alcohol until she died, and he paid for my schooling. Mother was right—he was Santa to me."

"Your real father," Jessie asked, "what happened to him?"

"Don't know. I never knew him. The only thing I was told was that he ran out of money."

"Well, then, Mac's perfect for you. He'll never run out of money."

"Mac isn't for me, Jessie. Mac's just a friend."

Jessie grinned. "You're the first person he's ever brought into our quarters, except Uncle Conner. I'd say he thinks of you as more than just a friend."

Sterling didn't have an answer for that. She turned to her lunch and pushed the half-touched plate of food away from her. Finally, Jessie stood and took the handles of Sterling's chair. "Guess I'd better get you back so I can get to class. I've already used up lunch hour and recess."

"Recess?"

"Yeah. Can you believe a college student having recess? That's Mrs. Everett for you, still living in the Dark Ages."

Sterling shook her head. She was still having trouble seeing Jessie as a college student. "Mrs. Everett's your teacher?"

"No, she's just my—my keeper. She's nice, but she just doesn't understand how lonely it gets around here. I wish . . . well, if wishes were horses . . ."

Later, back in her room, Sterling decided to learn how to operate her window to the world. She punched in the numbers to view her choices. The beach scene was nice. And she particularly liked the Parisian slide. A spring rain streaked the canvas, falling on artists scurrying to cover their work. Trees, heavy with blossoms, lined the sidewalks and the gutters. She could almost smell their blossoms. So romantic. So impossible.

The next scene was James Bond and his sex kitten. She studied Bond. He was a sophisticated man with a hint of the devil in his eyes, much too dashing for her.

And so was Mac. She started to sit down, then saw the tape.

Danish: the Words of Love in Six Easy Lessons.

Sterling groaned, picked up the tape, and threw it at the wall. "Take that, you . . . you smooth-talking man. Put it where your Danish is."

This time the tape struck James in a spot safely covered by a satin sheet. The sheet didn't help; the imagination was always more powerful than any projected image, no matter how realistic. In spite of her best attempt at focusing on James Bond, the man she was seeing was Mac.

Sterling's choice would have been to avoid the office for the afternoon. No, not avoid the office, avoid Mac. But when she finally talked to Conner, he informed her that he was indeed transferring her work to the mountain. Ten years of good work habits and responsibilities finally won out and she rolled herself back to Mac's hideaway.

He wasn't there.

Half-disappointed and half-relieved, she took her place at her computer and turned it on. Special orders and inquiries had backed up to an alarming degree, and she spent the better part of the afternoon answering E-mail messages. One of the messages she sent was to Conner. She didn't know how candid she could be on the Internet, so she settled for a simple *Please call me. Sterling.*

Work, she decided later as she returned to her quarters, was therapeutic. For four hours she'd avoided thinking about Vincent Dawson. She couldn't say the same about Lincoln McAllister.

As she rolled down the corridor she couldn't help feeling the vast emptiness around her. Little difference existed between Jessie and herself; neither left the secure cocoons in which they lived their lives. But then she realized that there was a difference. Her light, airy apartment and her office opened to the world, even if she didn't venture outside. Both were filled with constant visitors.

Here there was a constant hush, as if even the walls were holding their breath.

There was something unnerving about reaching a solid door and having it glide silently open before you as the one to her apartment had just done.

Inside, all the lights had been turned down to a soft glow. Music was playing. She didn't recognize the piece, but it was a haunting flute melody.

She rolled her shoulders, trying to relieve the tension that came from sitting before her computer. She longed to talk to Conner, but he hadn't returned her call yet. Her emotions bounced around like a pinball in one of those arcade machines.

In the bedroom she noticed that more clothes had been added to her meager wardrobe, among them a swimsuit. "Good idea," she said. "To whoever thought of it, thank you. A swim might be nice."

She wiggled out of her clothes, pulled on the suit, wincing at the brevity of the one-piece garment cut high at the thigh. But it was all she had. With the matching oversized towel slung over her shoulder, she wheeled herself to the rain forest.

It must surely be dark outside. Late December in New Mexico would bring nightfall early. Inside the pool area the lights had been lowered, but the sun was still shining. It was disconcerting. Glancing around, she couldn't see anyone, but there could be an army hidden in the thick greenery and she wouldn't know it. Almost reluctantly, she stood and walked to the pool, leaving her towel on one of the cushioned chaise longues.

Gripping the rocky ledge that lined the steps, she made her way carefully into the water. "Ahh." It was warm and inviting. The current rushing against her body at the base of the waterfall produced the same comfort and relief as the water jets in her Jacuzzi. She caught hold of a rail that ran around the rock, just under the surface, and floated there, allowing the plunging water to fall over her head and neck. It was heavenly.

The tension floated away, leaving her relaxed and sleepy. If she'd been in her bed, she would have fallen fast asleep. Grudgingly, she forced herself away from the waterfall and began to swim with long strokes, setting the steady pace she'd developed in the pool just outside her building. Up and down she swam, working out her mental exhaustion as the heated water unkinked her physical pain.

Morning and evening, no matter what, she'd forced herself to go to the pool. There'd been a time when all she could do was float. But gradually, as the feeling returned to her limbs, she'd begun to stretch her muscles. Now she did at least twenty-five laps twice a day.

Her entire life had changed yesterday, and yet it was the same. Here she had her work and the water. And in spite of the feeling of being in a kind of prison, she knew she was safe from Vincent Dawson.

Her mind flashed back to the screen of Bond and his blonde bed partner, except this time the woman in the bed was herself. Sterling blotted out the picture of the couple's entwined bodies. She wouldn't let her mind linger there.

The man standing in the shadows of the trees watched Sterling as she swam. He hadn't been surprised when she dropped her towel. He'd seen her body the night before. He'd felt her firm skin and wondered how she kept herself fit when she was so limited with her movements. Now he knew.

Her body cut a path through the plunging water, turned, and moved effortlessly with the current. How long had it been since he'd been in the pool? He found his exercise in the gym and in his morning meditations on a mountain ledge, shadowboxing with an imaginary foe.

Overhead, the timed control gradually lowered the lights as if the sun were setting. There wouldn't be stars overhead, but simulated moonlight was almost as good as the real thing.

Watching the woman instead of joining her definitely wasn't.

SEVEN

Mac watched Sterling leave the pool. Unaware that she was being observed, she leaned heavily on the rocks, wincing with every step. He had to force himself not to help her. A silent oath slipped through his lips. Spying on her was bad enough, offering his help would be the ultimate insult.

How had she managed to get away from Dawson at the airport? She'd walked a long way, not once but twice. Until now, he hadn't realized how difficult a simple movement was for her. He doubted that Conner knew the extent of her pain. No wonder she never left her building.

He could almost feel the agony. Experiencing such a personal connection to a woman was new and confusing. There was no reason for him to be drawn to Sterling, but he was. Though she claimed to be independent, that independence depended on someone else providing the kind of safe boundaries in which she could live alone. That dependence must rankle her, yet she didn't complain.

For most of his life he'd been surrounded by women who needed his help, beginning with Jessie's mother, Alice, who'd complained bitterly. Actually, he hadn't chosen Alice, at least not intentionally. She'd been chosen for him by his own irresponsibility and the fates. He'd done the right thing and married her. She'd been his wife but never his companion. He hadn't loved her, not the way a man ought to love the woman he married, and she'd known. But he respected her and cared for her. In the end, the death wish that raged inside her head had been more than she could control.

But she'd given him Jessie. Now Jessie, the sweet child who'd claimed his soul, was grown up. For so long she'd been unable to put her mother's death behind her, taking on the responsibility for it in ways even she didn't understand. With all the help and money he had at his disposal, he'd never known how to make her strong. He hadn't been able to save Alice. And Jessie's future was still to be defined. Becoming angel to the world had been safer than becoming angel to his family.

Now, he'd threatened his private sanctuary by bringing another woman who needed care into his life.

What made her different?

Her independence? Maybe, but he thought it was as simple as his genuine concern for her. During their telephone conversations over the years, he'd never formed a picture of the physical woman. He'd responded to her gentle voice and reassuring words. There'd been no expectations. They didn't know each other, so he could be himself. She never complained. She scolded him when he needed it, laughed at his silly jokes, offered a sympathetic ear when he just wanted to talk to someone who didn't judge him. He hadn't realized how emotionally attached he'd become to this woman.

Now that he'd met her, he'd learned that she was more than just bright, determined, and, in spite of her physical limitations, fiercely independent. She was a fighter who looked after herself, and if there were situations she couldn't handle, she avoided them.

That, apparently, included men.

Looking back, it was clear that from the first time they spoke on the phone, they'd made an immediate connection. Sparks flew. He just hadn't realized it until he touched her. That was the thing that stunned him. Desire came out of nowhere, and every time he was close to her, it grew.

The exterior Lindsey was as prickly as a spiny lizard, giving off don't-tred-on-me signals at every touch, yet underneath it all she hurt as much as he. He'd promised to help her when he'd sworn never to be responsible for keeping a woman safe again. He knew that kind of overwhelming responsibility. He'd failed once and he'd lived with that failure. He didn't think he could do that again.

When Sterling was in his office, Mac spent the

time driving his staff crazy. Though she hadn't asked for his help with her medical problems, he had his staff retrieving her records and researching her condition. Conner had assured him that Sterling's condition was irreversible, but Mac wanted to be certain.

Deep in his gut, he knew that he was building a nest for a woman who would likely fly away as soon as she was allowed. All this, when he should be worried about Vince Dawson. A stab of regret pierced him as Sterling coiled her damp towel into a turban around her hair and rolled herself out of view.

That regret suddenly became stark loneliness, an emotion he'd held at bay for a long time.

The door closed behind Sterling. He could see little wisps of fog rising from the pool as the heated water reached for the cool evening air near the ceiling. The beauty of the solarium still existed, but without someone to share it with, the artificial moonlight seemed cold.

Mac wasn't the only one who enjoyed Sterling's presence. Elizabeth liked her too. According to Burt, Jessie had spent several hours having lunch with Sterling. And they'd laughed. Burt—Mac smiled. Since Sterling's arrival, Burt had turned into a singing chef, bellowing operatic renditions in very bad Italian. Apparently, Sterling had brought out the lighter side of everyone.

Laughter in Shangri-la was rare.

Until Sterling.

❖————————❖

Vincent Dawson paced the balcony overlooking the senator's courtyard in New Orleans's Garden District. Vincent prided himself on his careful planning, covering all the possibilities, being prepared. What had happened ten years before had nearly cost him everything he'd worked for. Killing the securities broker had been necessary, though unplanned. The girl was a different matter.

Sterling Lindsey could have ruined him. Still could. The office was supposed to be empty; that had been the condition he'd insisted on with the old fool who thought he was dealing with a reclusive millionaire. The young woman's appearance in the office had been a surprise. She couldn't have identified him because of the ski mask, but he'd reacted before he'd thought. If the damned bullet had done the job, he wouldn't be in this mess right now. Instead of killing her, it had left her in a coma and paralyzed. Recovery had seemed unlikely. And when nothing had happened after she had recovered, he'd gotten lazy.

How in hell had this happened? What were the chances he'd run into her again? And what were the chances that she'd even recognize him? A million to one? Yet it had happened and it was apparent that in spite of the ski mask, she'd remembered. No doubt about that. He'd seen it in her eyes. Neither time, nor dyeing his hair, nor any other physical change had saved him from being identified.

And, even with all the men under his command, she'd gotten away. A woman in a wheelchair had managed to escape. But she'd had help. Given his political connections it hadn't taken long to identify her champion—Lincoln McAllister, the one man in the world who might be as powerful as Vincent Dawson. He started to pace, then turned and moved behind the desk Senator March had provided. The man seated in the chair opposite him was worried too.

"You know, going up against McAllister won't be easy," he said. "His complex has more security than Fort Knox. He has plenty of grateful friends in high places. And the amount of money he has at his disposal is unbelievable."

"Michael, you're in charge of security. I—the senator pays you for quiet solutions, not for problems. I don't accept that there is no way to penetrate this man-made fortress in the New Mexico mountains. I expect answers from you."

"We're working on it, Mr. Dawson. But our files are pretty complete. Shangri-la is impenetrable. McAllister is a genius."

"No place is impenetrable. We have the power of the United States government behind us. Use it!"

"The only way we'll get inside that mountain is to bomb it. Is that what you want?"

Yes, he started to say, then held back. From his desktop he picked up a paperweight. Inside the glass object was a medieval castle, complete with a moat.

Idly, he shook it, stirring up a miniature world of frothy snow.

"No, don't use force," he said. "I have an idea. If Muhammad won't come to the mountain, we'll have the mountain come to Muhammad. Thank you, Michael. Get Jonah for me."

"Jonah?" The seated man questioned. "Isn't that a bit extreme?"

"Not nearly as extreme as it's going to get."

Sterling found Mrs. Everett in her quarters after her swim. "Would you like to have dinner in the family dining room, or here in the apartment?" the older woman asked.

"Here, I suppose. I'm rather tired. But I feel bad about having someone cook for me. I really can prepare my own food."

"And deprive Burt of your compliments? He'd personally turn us both into shish kebabs. He's convinced you're a lady who appreciates good food."

Sterling looked down at her plump breasts, spilling over the top of the swimsuit. "That's what it looks like," she admitted. "He's right. I'll never look like the Danish babe."

"Excuse me? Danish babe?"

"Never mind. Say, would you care to join me?"

"I would, but I've already eaten. I'll send in a tray for you." She started to leave, then said earnestly, "I know you had lunch with Jessie today. I wonder . . . do you think she's . . . all right?"

A strange question to ask someone who met Jessie only twice, Sterling thought. "I'm not sure. I really don't know her very well. But, there is one thing."

"Yes?"

"Are you going to put up a Christmas tree?"

Elizabeth looked startled. "Well, no. We haven't done that in several years. It seemed to make the occasion sadder. But—why not? With you here it might work. I'll have one of the men get one. We have decorations around here somewhere."

"Wait. I'm not sure how long I'll be here. I mean . . . I wouldn't want to make false promises to Jessie. I told her that I'd be honest."

"Hmmph! I've thought for a long time that she's had enough truth. What she needs is a little make-believe." Elizabeth took a long look at Sterling. "Maybe that's what you need too."

The woman was right. "Mac too," she muttered under her breath.

The voice that answered was firm and a little amused. "Yep, Mac too."

The door closed.

Half an hour later the music began. Christmas carols were being piped through some kind of intercom system.

In the middle of "Santa Claus Is Coming to Town," there was a crackle, followed by Mac's voice. "By the way, Moneypenny, start making your list."

"What kind of list?" she said, wondering if he could hear her.

"For Santa. But I should tell you, Santa would rather you be naughty than nice. By the way, how're you doing on those Danish tapes?"

"Lincoln McAllister, are you watching me?"

"No. Would you like me to?"

"You know what I mean. Do you have some kind of hidden camera in this room." She stood and switched off all the lights.

"Sure. I tape all my guests' activities and use them for blackmail. How do you think I can afford all this?"

"Then you're out of luck. I'm in the dark and I have no money." She moved as fast as she could, pulling on a robe and combing the tangles from her hair.

"Well . . . we can fix that."

"What? You have infrared viewing?"

"No. I have money. And I have a deal for you. Will you forget about that tray in your room and have dinner with me? I want to talk to you about Jessie."

"About Jessie?"

"Jessie, my daughter. About Christmas."

"That's all? No Danish lessons?"

"Ah, Moneypenny. Everyone ought to learn a foreign language. Don't you know Bond never gives up?"

She smiled. "And Moneypenny never gives in."

"There's still time. Just throw on a robe and I'll pick you up in ten minutes."

"That's awfully quick. Where are you?"

"Right next door."

Why had he invited her to join him at dinner? He had initially planned on sharing a rare meal with Jessie, but she had already eaten.

The medical staff threatened him with amputation of certain parts of his anatomy if he stuck his head into their offices again. That seemed a bit extreme, at least the lower section of his body protested. He didn't have to be told twice to leave everyone alone. Mac needed someone to pass the time with, and Sterling was the perfect candidate.

Conner hadn't responded either to his pager or E-mail, and Mac knew that his Washington friends wouldn't appreciate him pressuring them any more than he already had. The soonest he was likely to hear anything was morning. The hours from now until then seemed an eternity.

When he'd sauntered into the kitchen and found Burt whistling merrily over his stove, he had no idea that he'd run straight into a trap. His innocent question—"What's for dinner?"—brought a lofty answer from Burtram Kazino, the man who owed his life to Mac but all his future earnings to a bookie who was probably still looking for a short-order cook.

"I'm preparing a special casserole for Sterling, nothing you'd like."

"Why do you say that?"

"Because you don't like casseroles. You always call them leftovers smothered with cheese and served with a strong wine so that you won't remember that you've already eaten it once."

Mac opened the door to the oven and took a sniff. "Doesn't smell like leftovers to me. Is there enough for two?"

"Actually, I'm preparing this for Ms. Lindsey. It's supposed to break the ice. Don't want the courtship to be too forward."

"Courtship? What do you mean *courtship*?"

"You've heard that the way to a man's heart is through his stomach?"

Mac nodded.

"Well, the way to a woman's is with a romantic meal; good food, good wine, and . . . *this*."

Burt opened the refrigerator and removed parfait glasses filled with vanilla and chocolate swirls. "And"—he grinned as he arranged the dessert on a tray—"if all else fails, bring her a gift." From beneath the counter he drew out a package wrapped in red foil and tied with a silver bow.

"Dare I ask what's in the box?"

"You do not. This gift isn't for you."

"You're really having dinner with Ms. Lindsey?" Mac asked, feeling a strange twinge of jealousy.

"I will be serving her, yes. And if you're going to join her, you'd better hurry."

"Me? But I thought—"

"You're always thinking, boss. When you gonna

stop that thoughty stuff and live dangerously. Tell her you'll pick her up in fifteen minutes. I've set a table in the library. I've selected the food and wine, you pick the music."

"But . . " Why was he being difficult? Having dinner with Sterling was exactly what he wanted to do. "Yes," he finally said. "I'll call her. And Burt, thanks."

He started out of the kitchen, a spring in his step that hadn't been there before. He bumped straight into Elizabeth, who was walking in. "Oh, Mac, I wanted to talk with you."

"Right now?" He'd didn't have time now. Minutes were ticking by. "I . . . I have an appointment. Can't it wait?"

"I suppose. Just answer one question. Sterling thinks that Jessie needs a more traditional Christmas. Do I have your permission to have a tree brought in?"

"Sure. And tell Jessie if she writes Santa a note, he might pay her a visit."

"Tell her yourself, Mac."

"I—I just might. It's been a long time since she sat on Santa's knee."

Elizabeth smiled as Mac moved out of the kitchen and down the hall whistling "Jingle Bells."

"What set him off?" she asked Burt.

"Don't know. Must be the casserole. Is it getting to you?"

Elizabeth eyed the chef skeptically. "What are you up to, you overgrown Cupid?"

"I'm sharpening my arrows, Lizzie, my girl. You'd better watch out. One of Santa's larger angels is watching you."

"And what is this *extra-large* angel planning to do?"

Burt took Elizabeth by the shoulders and backed her up to the door. "Look up, Lizzie?"

She did. In the archway, Burt had tied a tiny sprig of greenery full of white berries. "Now, Burt."

"Now, Lizzie, it's mistletoe. I haven't seen any mistletoe in the three years I've been here. I haven't kissed a pretty girl in too long, and I'll bet you haven't been kissed either."

"You aren't serious."

"Trust me, Lizzie, I am."

He was. And by the time he was finished, Lizzie knew exactly how deadly serious a kiss could be. She looked up at the man who towered over her. "You kissed me."

"That I did, and I intend to do it again. I've put this on top of my list of New Year's resolutions."

"But, Burt, I'm an old woman. I don't know what to say."

"Say you'll have dessert with me by the pool, and I'll tell you about all the gifts that Santa's bringing you."

A flush spread across her face. "I know you're going to think I'm silly, but I can't. I mean, I never . . . I shouldn't . . . what kind of dessert?"

"Chocolate kisses."

Too many years had passed since a man had looked at Elizabeth Everett as if she were the dessert. She swallowed hard and said a little prayer for forgiveness before she quipped, "I guess I could indulge in some dessert . . . just this once."

EIGHT

The Christmas music on Sterling's intercom faded. She had visions of Mac gleefully manipulating the buttons on some vast control board. And she wasn't certain that he wasn't watching her right now.

Without the music, the complete darkness smothered her. So be it. If Lincoln McAllister was a voyeur, and didn't get a good enough look the night he undressed her, he was about to see plenty. She turned the lights back on, and waited, expecting his voice to fill the silence.

Nothing.

Sterling didn't know whether she was pleased or angry.

Water from her wet hair ran down her face. She wiped her forehead, felt the sopping tendrils, and grimaced. Ten minutes? That's all the time she had to dress and turn herself into someone a man like 007 would want to face across a dinner table. It had been a long time since she'd even considered pleasing a man.

First, a dinner dress. She reminded herself to have Conner pack her own clothes and send them to her. They would make her feel less vulnerable.

As usual, Elizabeth had come up with something new. This time she'd laid out a long loose garment, half dressing, half evening gown. Made out of shimmering coral-colored material, the dress had a scooped elastic neckline and Empire bodice, from which the fabric was softly gathered.

Sterling looked around, picked up the clothing, and wheeled herself to her closet. Opening the door, she stood and stepped inside, where she ripped off the wet suit and donned the gossamer underwear Elizabeth had provided. She might as well not be wearing anything. The shape and color of her nipples were as obvious as if she were nude.

Before she panicked entirely, she pulled the gown over her head and threaded her feet into a pair of gold sandals that had appeared in her closet. Now, what on earth would she do about her hair?

Reclaiming her chair, she flipped the footrests down, wheeled herself into her bathroom, and replaced the wet towel around her head with a dry one that she spread over her shoulders. The hair dryer was already connected. She turned it on, let it get hot, and began to blow her hair. Once it started to dry, the heavy dark brown strands would turn into a mass of curls. She didn't have enough time to dry it completely. She'd just have to pull it back and fasten it with combs.

Laying the dryer aside for a moment, she turned to her makeup, applying moisturizer, followed by a natural base coat. A glittering taupe eyeshadow and mascara brought her eyes to life. The coral lipstick that she applied to her cheeks and her lips complemented the color of her gown.

She studied her efforts. A soft gasp escaped her lips. She looked like some kind of Grecian girl from days of old. All she needed was an urn.

There was a knock on her door.

"Just a minute." In her haste to turn her chair, she knocked her dryer to the floor and caught it in the wheel.

"Sterling? Are you all right? I'm coming in."

She heard the door open. "I'm in here."

"Oops! Are you decent?"

"Certainly. I just dropped my dryer. It's pretty useless, my hair's a mess."

"Your hair is . . ." His voice trailed off.

She looked up, meeting his eyes in the mirror. "I'm sorry, Mac. All my things were in my case and it got lost somewhere along the way. Mrs. Everett has done the best she could, but I would never dress like this."

"You should," he said. "You're lovely. But if these things don't suit you, Elizabeth will take you shopping and you can replace anything you need."

"I know, you have a store here in the mountain."

"A small one. What we don't have, the manager brings in."

"What I need right now is a hairdresser."

"Sorry, we don't have one handy." He picked up the dryer. "Will I do? I used to dry Jessie's hair." He turned the appliance on and began to direct the stream of heat beneath her hair, pulling it out and combing it with his fingertips.

The effect was hypnotizing. In the mirror she could watch his cool concentration, the way he massaged her scalp as he separated the strands. The feathery touch of his hands fanned the hotness of the blown air. Overhead, the mirror was beginning to fog over and she wasn't entirely certain that it was from the dryer.

"Mac, that's fine. I can manage now."

He paused and caught her gaze in the mirror. "I know you can manage, but I can do it much quicker. Just close your eyes and let me. Please?"

How could she refuse? There was something mesmerizing about his touch, about feeling the warm air against her skin as he lifted the hair, exposing it to the heat section by section. She closed her eyes and once more forced herself to relax.

Finally, he laid the dryer on the counter, giving her hair one last touch, then stepped away. "I think that's it."

She opened her eyes to find a different woman looking back at her. He hadn't used a curling iron to shape her hair and the result was a mass of fine curls, capping her head like a lacy veil.

"Mac. I look like some kind of . . . I don't know. Wild child. Maybe one of those flower children from the sixties."

He put his hands on her shoulders and leaned forward so that the two faces in the mirror were side by side.

"Were you ever a wild child?"

"Not really. I was too sensible, too busy preparing myself to be the CEO of General Motors."

"That's what I thought. Tell you a little secret, Sterling. I was wild enough for both of us."

"I'll bet you had long hair and rode a Harley."

"If you'd put money on that bet, you'd be a rich woman. A Harley, a Porsche, a vintage convertible, and a Palomino stallion. If it cost money, I had it. If it went fast, I raced it."

And if it needed loving, she'd bet he loved it. She wanted to respond with something light, as they had before, but the tension between them left her speechless.

Finally, Mac straightened up. "I think we're looking at two deprived people. Maybe we'd better see what Burt is serving before he comes after us with one of his long-handled forks."

Sterling felt a slow blush steal across her face. What on earth had gotten into her? She'd been staring into that mirror like some kind of lovestruck girl, caught up in the fantasy of a lover who brushed her hair. Of being a wild child.

She was safer with the holograph of Bond and

the Danish babe. It was only a picture. What she'd been caught up in moments ago was real.

Too real.

"Yes," she managed to say. "I'm starving." She looked down at herself; the neckline of her Grecian gown was far too low. Her ample breasts were threatening to spill over and a tug at the top only made Mac aware of her discomfort. "Swimming always increases my appetite," she finished lamely, and folded her wrists in her lap.

"Do you swim much?"

"Every day. Sometimes twice a day. Your pool is lovely. Do you use it?"

"Not much," he admitted. "Jessie does. I built it for her, to exercise her legs."

They'd gone only a short distance down the corridor when Mac stopped and waited. A light came on over the door and it opened silently.

"Magic?" she teased.

"No. Photo identification again. Toys. Every time my engineers hear about something new, they have to try it. It's part of my research lab."

"Technology is a wonderful thing."

"Yes, but there are some things it still can't do."

She heard a wistfulness in his voice. "Is that why you don't sleep at night?" She should have bitten her tongue. The connection between them had lessened. The last thing she needed to bring up was something that tied them together personally.

"How'd you know about my being an insomniac?"

"You always called me after midnight, remember?"

He looked down for a moment. "And you were always there."

"Yes, I had my share of sleepless nights. You know why I was awake. What about you?"

"So many things keep me from sleeping, Sterling. I think we both have our own demons. Now that I know about Vincent Dawson, I understand one of your demons better."

She could have corrected him, told him that Vincent Dawson's eyes were only one thing that haunted her at night. Until now she might have blamed him for all of it. She would have been fooling herself. In those dark lonely hours when the shadows reached out and pulled her in, it was human contact that she needed and found in the voice of a stranger.

Now that stranger was real and she was having a hard time dealing with being so close to him. A voice in the darkness filled those empty spaces, but it disappeared in the light.

"I hope you don't mind," Mac said, "but Burt set a table in my quarters."

"Your quarters?"

"I told you. I'm next door, remember?"

She remembered.

His apartment was almost Spartan in its decor. There were rough, sand-colored walls, simple furniture of a light-colored wood, and rugs that resembled Indian blankets. From the foyer she could see a fireplace in the living room that might be found in any adobe house in the Southwest.

Sterling looked around in amazement, then over her shoulder at Mac. "It's lovely. Does the fireplace work?"

"Of course. There's another one in the library where Burt set up our table. Would you like a fire?"

"I'd love a fire."

He moved her chair through the doorway into a small room lined with books. Several overstuffed cream-colored couches nestled around a larger fireplace already bright with glowing coals.

"Looks like Burt already decided we needed one," Mac said.

This time there was no holograph, no window opening on the outside world. Instead, the lights were low, supplemented by thick white candles ringed with poinsettias in the middle of the table.

"It's lovely. I can see why you never leave Shangri-la. You have everything you want right here."

He stopped the chair for a moment, allowing her to take in the setting Burt had created. "Almost. Almost. Can you stand? I think you'd be more comfortable in the chairs Burt arranged."

"Of course. I told you I can walk. Short distances are fine; it's the long treks that hurt." She leaned down to fold the footrests up.

"Let me." He made a move toward her feet.

"No!" she said sharply, then raised up, regretting the sharpness of her voice. "I'm sorry. It's just that since I left the rehabilitation center, I've never had anyone so . . . close."

"What about Conner?"

She laughed as she pushed herself up. "His stealth in the marines might have given him his nickname—The Shadow—but when it comes to nursing, he has two left feet. Seriously, it took a long time, but I don't think he sees me as handicapped anymore. There are times when I have to remind him that I can't climb mountains or swim oceans."

Mac helped her into her chair and pushed it beneath the crisp white tablecloth. Then he moved the wheelchair and turned to the wine cabinet. "Looks like Burt has chosen the wine. I hope you like this one. I have it sent in from France."

"I can't say that I'm a connoisseur. I—I don't drink much. For so long being clearheaded was more important than satisfying my taste buds."

Mac filled her wineglass then his own. As he sat down he raised his glass. "A toast, Sterling. To Bond and Moneypenny, two lost souls together at last."

She smiled and touched her glass to his. "No, Mac. To Sterling and Mac, two lost souls trapped in a mountain by a madman."

He sipped his wine. "I liked my toast better."

"Mine is more honest."

"All right, then. Accepting that honesty is the best policy. Tell me about yourself?"

"Myself? You already know more about me than anybody else has ever known, including Conner."

"I don't mean the accident. Tell me about the

woman who was going to be the CEO of General Motors."

"She's been gone so long, I'm not sure I even remember her anymore."

"That's probably just as well. Most of the corporate women I've dealt with are alligators." He glanced across the table at her and smiled. "I like flower children better."

"I might, too, but I'm afraid I don't fit into that category either. My life is pretty much Paradox, Inc. I run Conner's company, not the actual business part of it. There are warehouses and accountants for that. I deal more with the overall picture. He needs a product and I find it. He wants to sell something unique and I find a buyer. If someone needs him to do something, I facilitate it."

"And you look after him," Mac said softly.

"I did. Now he has Erica. I'm having to learn to step back and let her claim the man she married."

The fire crackled in the silence.

"That must be hard," Mac said. "I've never had to let go—except once. I've always been more concerned with shoring up."

"You sound like you're talking about buildings, not people."

"I guess I am. Being close to people isn't something I'm comfortable with. Would you like some music?" he asked, abruptly changing the subject.

"Am I going to get another chorus of 'Santa Claus Is Coming to Town'?"

He stood and moved over to an entertainment

center on the wall just inside the door. "Not if you've made your list?"

"No list," she said. "I expect Santa to know what I want. It's the same thing I've asked for every year."

He hit a button and the sweet voice of Celine Dion sang softly through the room. He listened for a moment, then said, "If you didn't get what you asked for, maybe you're asking for the wrong thing."

She thought of her childish request for someone to love her and nodded. "I think you're absolutely right. That's why I stopped asking."

There came a knock on the door.

"You decent, Mac?" It was Burt.

"Of course I'm decent."

"Too bad. In that case, I'm coming in." The rotund chef rolled a serving cart into the room. "Evening, ma'am. I'm sorry, you must have taken the wrong turn. I'm supposed to be serving Ms. Lindsey, not a model from the Victoria's Secret catalog."

Sterling gasped. "Is that where this dress came from?"

Burt leaned closer and studied her. "Golly, it *is* Sterling. Sorry, ma'am. I didn't recognize you."

"I'm not surprised," she said, tugging once more at the neckline of her gown. Apparently, it really was a gown, not a dinner dress. She'd been on the lingerie company's mailing list for years, but she never ordered anything. Her normal sleepwear was an oversized T-shirt and cotton underpants—not the sensual underwear she was wearing tonight.

"The food Burt?" Mac frowned at his employee.

"Sorry, boss. I know you've had your mouth set for eggplant-and-onion casserole ever since you smelled it in the kitchen."

Sterling bit back a smile as Burt placed fine china bowls filled with a creamy tomato soup before them.

"I hope you like the meal, Sterling." Burt winked. "The company I can't guarantee, but I tried to prepare something that would make the evening special."

He winked at Mac. "I'll just leave the rest of the serving to you, boss. There's room underneath for the plates. The casserole is warming and the dessert is on the cart." He backed out, reached for the door, and lowered the lights even more.

"Don't forget your surprise, boss," he said. "I put it on the cart for you."

Sterling took a sip of her soup and sighed. "If everything is as good as this soup, I'm in trouble."

Mac tasted the soup. "If you follow Burt's advice, you may be in more trouble than you think."

"Oh? Why is that?"

"First, he's late. Second, his jacket was only half-buttoned. And third, unless he's not feeling well, he's taken to wearing lipstick?"

The clink that followed was Sterling's soupspoon landing in her bowl. "Burt?"

Mac grinned. "Never knew Burt to let anyone in his kitchen but family and—Elizabeth." The grin widened. "Imagine that. Elizabeth and Burt. Do you think?"

Sterling didn't want to think. The soft candlelight, the romantic music, and the evening Burt was orchestrating didn't need any thought.

"Now, about that alligator," Mac said. "Tell me more about how she turned into the lady I'm fantasizing about."

"Mac, don't do that. I'm no man's fantasy. I put that kind of life behind me long ago."

"Why?" he asked curiously.

She looked at him with a touch of irritation. "That should be obvious."

"What's obvious is that you're a woman who doesn't have a clue about how beautiful she is."

Sterling blotted her lips with her napkin and placed her spoon in her empty bowl. "Please, don't do this, Mac."

"Do what?"

"Tease me. I'm having enough trouble dealing with what happened. I've been moved away from my home and forced to face the possibility that I may not come out of this whole thing alive. That tends to make a person vulnerable. And now you're . . . you're making me uncomfortable with your . . . flirting."

He tensed. She was right. What was he doing? Sitting across from Sterling, he was as excited as a teenager and he was only making it worse with his suggestive conversational gambits.

Without thinking, he slid his hand over, covering hers. A new bolt of desire connected them and she stared at him. There was fear in her eyes, uncertainty, and the kind of naked need that couldn't be denied. It wasn't just him. It wasn't something that either could turn on and off as though it didn't exist.

"Sterling." He stood and moved around the table. "I don't think I like this any more than you, but damned if I want to stop it. You're right, I've been lonely. I've just had to learn to live with it."

She stood, pushing her chair back. "With the airport and *that* man, everything changed and I don't know how to change it back."

Then she was in Mac's arms, strong arms that supported her and pulled her close. No, she didn't—couldn't want this.

Mac groaned. "Sterling . . ."

Then he brushed her lips and she knew that this was what she'd wanted from the first time he'd touched her. It was a shock to realize that she was so ready, so willing. As his lips touched hers she stopped fighting her desire and caught her fingertips in the buttons of his shirt, drawing him closer. He wasn't a great deal taller than she, but she was forced to tilt her head slightly to allow him access to her mouth. He lingered there, then moved to her eyes.

"I slept last night," she whispered. "And I dreamed about you. I never have dreams like that. And I don't want to."

She felt his heart beating against her fingers. This wasn't supposed to be happening. There was an intensity about him that said he was no more in control of his actions than she was in control of hers.

She was way out on a limb here and she didn't seem to be able to get back.

His lips scrubbed her cheeks. "You shouldn't have to dream about me wanting you. It ought to be real."

"What are you saying?"

"I think we've talked enough, Sterling."

"No."

He kissed her neck. "Are you sure?"

"No! I . . . I mean, yes."

"Good. Talking isn't what I have in mind."

NINE

"Put me down, Mac! I can walk."

"Shut up, Sterling."

He kissed her again. This time the kiss wasn't gentle. It was rough, demanding, and it turned her mind to mush. He needed her. And tonight she needed to be needed. For so long she'd been afraid. Years had passed before she'd realized that she had suppressed any thought of physical desire and now it roared through her like an out-of-control fire.

"What are you doing?"

"Carrying you off to bed."

"But—but—I don't . . . I mean, we can't. I don't . . . speak Danish," she muttered inanely.

He pulled back and looked at her. Her words brought a grin to his face. "Trust me, Sterling, language skills don't matter."

Mac strode into his bedroom and to the bed. "Lights on. Dim," he said, and let her feet slide to the floor. Moments later the Victoria's Secret gown was gone, as was Mac's shirt and shoes. He jerked his socks from his feet, unzipped his jeans, then paused and looked up at Sterling.

He groaned.

"Where did Elizabeth get that underwear?"

"Burt was right. The labels say Victoria's Secret."

"Remind me to arrange for an outlet here."

He reached out with one finger, rimming the dusky rose of her nipples through the thin fabric of her bra.

Slyly, she copied him, running her finger along the elastic edge of his briefs. "Since I don't get out much, I haven't shopped at one of their stores. Aren't most of their customers men?"

"If their models look like you, I'd say men are their best customers."

She hesitated. "I doubt they'd hire me. The women I see in the fashion shows are very tall and thin."

He unhooked her bra and let it fall forward, freeing her full breasts. "If that's true, just think how much their sales would increase if they hired you."

Under his intense gaze, she was beginning to shiver. Another minute with Mac and she would lose all self-control. That is, if she had any to begin with, when he was near her.

He clasped her tightly with one arm and pulled back the cover. After that she didn't know what happened, only that her panties and his briefs were gone and he was leaning over her. They were touching, every inch of them sliding against the other's corresponding parts. Touching, kissing, exploring until she felt herself urging him closer.

Spreading her legs, he nestled down between them and then, still kissing her, he was inside her. Her body instinctively tightened around him. It had been so long since she'd felt such hot, urgent need. So long since she'd felt connected with a man. No connection had ever felt like this. When he raised himself, she followed, unwilling to let him go. When he descended, she pressed herself against him and felt her nerve endings start to explode.

The rapid breathing, the moaning; she didn't know if it was Mac or her. The ever-intensifying heat. The release that sent her spinning into another dimension.

And then he collapsed on top of her, unable to move.

For a long time he lay there, waiting for his muscles and nerves to return to life. A heartbeat threatening to send him straight to the emergency room of the nearest hospital finally began to slow.

"I'm sorry," he said, and slid to the side, rolling to his back. "Did I hurt you?"

"Hurt me?" she whispered, wondering, with her vow of honesty, whether or not to tell him that she thought he probably had, though not physically. "No," she whispered. "I'm fine."

"You're sure. I mean, I was pretty rough on you and it's been a long time."

"Could you tell?"

"I couldn't tell you what day of the week it is right now, Sterling. I mean I was so aroused that I might have . . " He slipped his arm beneath her head and drew her close. "I don't know what to say."

Sterling didn't know what to say either. She thought it would be the woman who was speechless after an orgasm, not the man.

"So, what did we just prove?" she finally asked.

"We proved that you're a very sensual woman," Mac answered, realizing the inadequacy of his reply.

"And you're a very sensual man. But I didn't have to sleep with you to know that."

"Is that what you call it, sleeping with me?"

"Well, yes. Except that we haven't done any sleeping yet. Perhaps it would be more appropriate if I called it making out or—" Any of the more modern terms, she couldn't bring herself to say.

Mac pulled away and sat up. The questions in her eyes told him that she was as uncomfortable as he. *You wanted her, McAllister. You took her. She went with you and that's what you needed. Why do you feel like you've deflowered a virgin?* "I'm sorry, Sterling. I shouldn't have done that."

Sterling closed her eyes, concealing the confusion his withdrawal had caused. Had she been such a disappointment? She couldn't believe that, but considering the extent of Mac's experience, she might not know.

"I didn't think beyond the moment," he said, his voice dropping to a low mumble.

"I could have stopped you," she said.

"I know you don't believe me, but I don't usually do this."

"I know I'm the first woman you've brought to the family quarters."

He looked over his shoulder, voicing a question with his eyes.

"Jessie told me. I tried to assure her that you were simply protecting me. Are you, Mac?"

"From everyone but me."

He stood and walked to the foot of the bed, where he found his underwear and stepped into it.

"Why are you angry, Mac?"

"I'm not," he snapped.

"That sounds like anger to me."

It was, but not at her. At himself, for his lack of control, and inability to reassure her. Hell, he himself didn't even know how he felt. How could he tell her?

"I . . . I'm hungry," he finally said, settling for blunt assertion rather than the light banter they'd exchanged during tense moments earlier. "Another minute and my stomach is going to growl."

It was one of his defense mechanisms, the kind in which a person locks onto something totally idiotic to say in order to cover up his or her real feelings. Even Mac realized it as soon as he'd spoken. A forced smile curled his lips and he came back to the bed and sat beside Sterling.

For a long time he just looked at her. "I guess

you had to learn about my bad temper sooner or later."

"I guess you had to learn about my weakness sooner or later."

"Your weakness?"

She had to come up with something to explain her bizarre behavior.

"Avoidance. For me," she improvised, "sex is like eating banana ice cream. Some people probably don't like it. I don't always like it. But every now and then I feel an uncontrollable urge for bananas."

"And what do you do to control those urges?"

"I don't allow banana ice cream in my house. Avoidance. That's what I mean. There are some things I simply can't refuse, so I avoid them."

"Are you comparing banana ice cream to me or to—sex?"

She grew serious. "I think I may be comparing it to the truth. If my temptation is something I can't deal with, I avoid it." She pulled the sheet over her breasts. "I'd like to get dressed now, Mac."

This brief moment of honesty somehow reassured him. Still heavy-lidded from lovemaking, she was so beautiful. "Don't suppose you'd let me help?"

"No, thank you. I can do it myself. If you'll just let me wrap this sheet around me, I'll—"

"Dash down the corridor to your room and run straight into Jessie? I don't think so. You know children don't expect their parents to have sex."

"Parents don't expect their children to have sex either, but they do. Besides, Jessie is no child."

"I know," he said sadly. "That's what I wanted to talk to you about, but I guess that can wait until later."

"All right." She made a move to rise.

"Please. I think you'd better stay here, Sterling. Besides, our dinner is waiting. Burt planned it and I don't want to face him if we leave it untouched."

"Mac, I don't think I have an appetite for casserole right now?"

He gave her a prolonged look and laid his hand on her hip, feeling the soft curves beneath the sheet. For a moment he didn't move. Then his fingers began to gather the sheet in rumpled handfuls as he moved up her chest. By the time he reached her breasts, the sheet was gone and dusky red nipples beaded like large cherries beneath his touch.

"Neither do I. But I can't let you go like this."

Why was she pretending? Nobody had to tell her that this night would be the first and last time that Mac made love to her. This was her evening to feel like a woman and she closed off any reservations by taking his head in her hands and pulling it down to her breast. "I don't think I can leave now anyway."

His lips suddenly left her breasts and captured her mouth. Her hand slid around his upper arm, urging him on. And then he was turning to lie down beside her, supporting himself on one arm while he pulled her closer. Bare legs tangled in the bedcovers. She could feel him hard against her. It was incredibly erotic. Everything about Lincoln McAllister was erotic. His strong manly scent; the slight scratch of his beard, light, yet coarse; the hair on his chest that became a thousand tiny fingers dancing across her breasts.

The pain that was always present in her back and legs disappeared. It had been instantly erased during the explosive release of their first climax. Now she felt as though she were flying through space.

Finally he slowed down and pulled back, looking at her with eyes that had become almost black with emotion. "Sterling, you're a witch. I can't be close to you without touching you."

"You're just starved for sex," she joked. "Any safe port in a storm."

"This is a storm all right. Every part of me is churning"—he thrust his lower body against her thigh—"but I don't think I have to tell you that."

Her chest was tight. She could barely speak. "No. You don't."

"How do you feel about this—us? Is it going to be a problem for you?"

This was the big question. What was her answer? What could she say? That she was torn between her desire for another chance at love, and her uncertainty and fear that he was just another man who would walk out on her. She wasn't fooling herself. There was nothing permanent in this; Mac hadn't even pretended that there would be. She respected him for that.

"Sterling?"

Just as she'd told Jessie, she'd tell Mac the truth. "A problem? Probably. I'm thirty-two years old and I've had only one real relationship, my fiancé, Allen. The engagement ended when I was shot. Not instantly, of course; it took a while. Before that I wasn't a virgin. Who was in the eighties? After Allen, there was only one time and I guess you'd say it was for medicinal purposes."

He frowned. "Medicinal purposes?"

"For a long time, I thought I'd never be a woman again, never be able to do anything.

"Then I met this man and he made the think differently about myself. One man, one time. A therapist."

"The one you replaced with a woman?"

"Yes. He showed me that I could have a life with a man. I just . . . never have since."

His hand found her breast once more and played with it absently, pausing now and then to rim it with his tongue.

"Remind me to check on our staff therapist. I hadn't heard about that part of the recovery process." Mac's attention was diverted as she slid her hand beneath the sheet. She touched his stomach, then moved lower. "Mac?"

He moaned. "Sterling, what I was about to say—"

"Like you said earlier, Mac, no more talking."

This time there was no awkwardness after their lovemaking. He simply pulled her close and kissed her. The lights, already low, went even lower. "What about Burt's casserole?" he finally asked.

"It's probably ruined?"

"Good. I don't like casseroles anyway. We'll flush it down the toilet."

"Are you still hungry?"

"Yes, but I'm too wiped out to move. I'm an old man, lady. I can't do this kind of thing all night."

She laughed. "How old are you, Mac?"

"Will you get up and run if I tell you that I'm forty-two?"

"I couldn't get up and run if you told me you were an ax murderer. Just a figure of speech," she amended. "I couldn't run, period."

He lay silent for a time. "What I was trying to tell you earlier was that I was so—I don't know any other way to say it—aroused that I wasn't prepared."

"If you were surprised, double it and you'll know how I felt."

"You don't understand, Sterling. I can't say that I've kept myself as pure as you, but I've always protected myself and the women I've made love to."

"I believe you."

"Until tonight. Listen to what I'm saying. I didn't use any protection, either time. I ought to be castrated."

She thought about what he'd said and blushed. She was glad that he couldn't see. The blush was more than just embarrassment that he hadn't even thought about it, but that she hadn't.

"That might be a bit extreme," she said. "Mac,

when two people have sex, both of them are responsible for what happens."

"But you're . . . you're—"

"If you say handicapped, I'll reconsider your punishment. I'm so relaxed that my bones are Jell-O. My body is saying yum, yum. The only thing I want to do right now is close my eyes and float."

"Then float, Sterling. But sooner or later we're going to have to talk."

"You talk. I'll listen." She closed her eyes.

Before Mac could worry anymore, she was sound asleep, pressed against him as if his body had been perfectly shaped to conform to hers. He understood what she meant about floating. Even the knowledge that he'd failed to reach inside the drawer to his nightstand didn't cause him great distress. The truth was, there was nothing there. He'd never needed it here before.

Sterling moaned softly and readjusted her position, throwing her leg over his, so that he could feel the soft down of hair brushing his thigh. Forty-two years old or not, his manhood was announcing its youth. Instantly erect and tight with the burgeoning of a desire that seemed to intensify instead of dissipate upon receiving gratification.

"Ah, darling," he whispered, capturing a full breast in his hand, "I may have just given you more proof of your womanhood than that young therapist. For the second time in my life my uncontrolled desire may have given a woman a child. And this time, even after I knew what I'd done, I loved you again."

As the night waned Mac thought about the consequences of his actions. The one thing he steadfastly refused to do was question why.

The ring of the phone pierced the silence like a shot.

Mac reached for it, felt the unexpected weight on his arm, and shook his head in sleep. Sterling. She was still lying across him.

"What is it?" Her voice was thick with sleep.

"The phone. Go back to sleep."

But as he reached for the phone she sat up.

"Mac here."

"Mac," came the voice of Mrs. Everett, "sorry to disturb you, but you didn't tell me not to."

"Why shouldn't you disturb me?"

"Well . . . I thought . . . I mean, you aren't alone."

"Just tell me what's so important at this hour of the night."

"It's after ten o'clock in the morning and there's an urgent call for you."

"Ten o'clock? Damn! From who?"

"Conner Preston."

Mac swung his feet to the floor and sat up. "Please put him through, Elizabeth." He looked at Sterling. "Will you excuse me, Sterling."

"That depends," she said, tucking the sheet beneath her breasts as she leaned against the headboard. "On whether or not the conversation concerns me."

"I can take it in my office," he said, "but I'd rather not have to do that."

Sterling slid to the foot of the bed and stood, wrapping the sheet around her. "You won't have to," she said, and left the room, waves of anger rippling away from her path.

Mac sighed. "What's up, Conner?"

"I hope I'm not interupting. Mrs. Everett seemed to think I might be."

"Mrs. Everett isn't my mother. What's wrong?"

"We intercepted a message. It seems our Mr. Dawson has sent for Jonah, a paid assassin."

"A paid assassin? I don't like that."

"Neither do I. The conference call for our team is set for one o'clock. Will you—will you be free by then?"

"Free? Of course I'll be free. I'm heading for the office now."

"What about Sterling? Are you going to include her?"

"Sterling will not be involved in the conference call, Conner. The less she knows, the better."

Conner didn't answer for a moment. "Hmm. Correct me if I'm wrong, but isn't she listening?"

"Of course not!" Mac sputtered.

"I don't think she's gonna like that, Mac."

"She could be killed, Conner. What's wrong with you?" He dropped the handset quietly back into its cradle. What had Mrs. Everett told Conner?

Why in hell had he put monitoring and identification systems into the computer? At the time it had seemed logical that they be able to track everyone in the mountain. He'd never considered that the system might track a woman to his bed.

His bed. It was empty. Emptier than it had ever been before. Even Sterling's clothes were gone. He didn't know what she had heard if any of the conversation or how much of it she understood. Worse, he didn't know what he could do to make this right. He swore again and padded to the bathroom, picking up his clothes as he went. He didn't know where his briefs had gotten to this time, probably under the covers at the foot of the bed. Well, just let Elizabeth find them when she hustled in to tidy up. He'd hired a maid for that, but she insisted on doing his personal things herself. Maybe this would stop her.

He stuffed his clothes in the hamper, kicked the corner of the bed, and changed the light switch to sunlight.

Glancing around once more, he decided that it was time to redecorate. The room was too severe. It felt cold.

Sterling wasn't in it.

TEN

Sterling just couldn't believe it! Mac, the man she'd just spent the night with, the man she'd shared her life's story with and to whom she'd explained her need for independence, was leaving her out of the loop. It was too much.

After listening to Mac's conversation outside the doorway, Sterling grew furious. She tucked the sheet around her, commanded Mac's bedroom door to open, almost crushing a small package with a large card marked *Sterling* on it with her foot. She reached down, tucked the package under her arm, and strode down the hall. If she encountered Jessie, so be it. Jessie wasn't a child. She was just sheltered, like Sterling had been. It was time something made her want to leave the mountain. It didn't have to be a murder to do it.

Spending the last ten years inside the Paradox building had been Sterling's way of dealing with an uncertain world. She'd been safe and she'd become more successful in her career than she'd ever dreamed. How many women were on a first-name basis with prominent art dealers and collectors, heads of state, buyers and sellers of rare and exclusive merchandise? How many women controlled the amount of money that she did? And then again, how many women had no one to share their lives, their dreams, or their futures with?

She'd always had Conner. He was her family. But now he was married to Erica and his priorities were already changing. She'd decided to find a new job, a new career, a new apartment. Since returning to her own apartment would only put her in Vincent Dawson's clutches.

What did it matter now since he was coming here to get her? She needed to know when and how.

Minutes later she was back in her own quarters. But she'd been so incensed that she'd walked, the pain in her heart stronger than that in her legs. Her wheelchair was still in Mac's bedroom.

So be it. Apparently everyone knew what had happened. She took a quick shower, dressed, and headed for the office Mac had set up for her. Once inside, she turned back to face the open door. "Close and lock," she said. The doors complied. At least they closed; she had no way of knowing whether or not they were locked.

For the rest of the morning she learned how to operate the new computer Mac had installed. Mac had tied the files of Paradox into the main operation for the complex. With the hours Sterling had spent learning how to interface internationally, she was able to find a way to Mac's conference call. She had no doubt that Mac would know when she gained access, but what could he do?

The holographic screen on the opposite wall was suddenly filled with Mac, sitting behind his desk. For a moment he looked startled, then angry.

"Gentlemen, it looks as if Ms. Lindsey has joined us. Sterling, I trust you will remain silent if I allow you to remain on-line."

Sterling wanted to scream. If he *allowed* her? She counted to five, took a deep breath, and said as sweetly as she could manage, "Good afternoon, gentlemen. Thank you for your concern on my behalf. Go ahead, Mr. McAllister. I'm listening. If you need to know anything from me, just ask."

"General Scott here." The screen changed to the speaker, a bald man with enough medals to impress even Sterling, a woman not easily impressed. "All right, what's the problem, Mac?"

"First, let's meet the team," Mac said. "You know General Scott. We are also joined by a friend we'll call only Daniel. You'll understand if we don't show his face. Daniel is an expert on international crime and on the criminals who operate from the shadows."

The screen changed to the silhouette of a man sitting in front of a window. The bright sunlight behind him effectively disguised his features.

They received only a nod from Daniel.

Mac continued, "And there's Burt, who knows more about the underworld in our own country than J. Edgar Hoover ever did."

Sterling jumped when a shot of their own chef, Burt appeared. "Sterling, sweetie," he chided, "you didn't eat your casserole or the breakfast I sent this morning. But I forgive you."

Sterling blushed. Burt couldn't see her face, but by now, he and every one at Shangri-la probably knew she'd spent the night in Mac's bed.

"You remember Raymond, my assistant and chief of security. And finally, I think you all know Conner. I'll let him explain what we've learned."

Conner's dear face appeared, lined and haggard. "Afternoon, all. Sterling, it would be better if you didn't know what we're doing. It could put you in more danger."

"If I'm in danger—" Her image suddenly flashed on the screen. She was surprised to see that she didn't look tired at all. In fact, she glowed as if she'd just reached into her Christmas stocking and discovered new legs. "I think I'm entitled to know what you're doing and why. Explain, Conner."

Conner smiled and shook his head. "All right. Here's the skinny. Vincent Dawson, personal adviser and aide to Senator March from Louisiana, has been identified by my assistant as the man who shot her employer and wounded her ten years ago."

The general: "Preposterous. Even political advisers have to pass a security check."

Conner continued. "Because he was never identified, never charged, he has no criminal record. The only blot on his background is the possibility of a 'relationship' with Congresswoman Gardner, his former employer." Conner described the congresswoman's will, Dawson's inheritance, and the subsequent lawsuit, then moved on.

"On the surface, Vince is as clean as a whistle. He apparently converted the bearer bonds to a fictitious name and cashed them in and funneled the proceeds into his account as needed, under the guise of income earned. He could then buy his way into a major role in March's campaign for the Senate. Since then he has very quietly become a very powerful man in Washington."

"Sterling," Mac said, "do you want to tell us about your encounter with Mr. Dawson?"

"Ten years ago I was interning with an investment and securities firm." She explained about the phony millionaire's appointment to buy bearer bonds and how she interrupted the thief as he was emptying the safe. "My employer was murdered and I was shot and left for dead."

"And the police never found the killer?" Burt asked.

"For a long time I was in a coma. I couldn't give them much of a description. I was a temporary employee. The police thought he must have had inside help. Then when I told them he was wearing a ski mask, the police didn't believe me."

The general interrupted. "You didn't see him,

but you've now decided that Vincent Dawson is that man. On what basis?"

"His eyes," Sterling said calmly. "They are very unusual, something like a mottled blue-gray marble. I saw his lips and I heard his voice. Gentleman, it was Mr. Dawson. I am certain of that."

"As I was about to say," Conner explained, "he and Sterling met in the New Orleans airport. Once he saw her, he sealed off the airport and began a search. There was no reason for his action, if he hadn't recognized her."

"And," Sterling added, "he knew I recognized him."

Burt came onscreen. "So, even if we have a positive identification, it wouldn't hold up in court."

The man in the shadows hadn't spoken, until now. "The last thing Dawson wants is the publicity. He's a very powerful man with a reputation to protect. He won't go public and neither can we."

"We know," Mac said seriously, "he's called in Jonah."

There was a long silence.

"Sterling," Conner began, "Jonah is—"

"I know, a paid assassin. I appreciate all of your concern, but I don't think you can fix this." She thought about Erica and the baby and Conner. "I won't have any of you put yourselves at risk for me. I disappeared ten years ago, and with your help, I can do that again. It's the only way."

"She could be right," Burt said.

"Maybe so," Conner agreed.

Mac nodded. "Once Dawson finds out that she's out of it, he'll be forced to move on."

What none of them was saying, Sterling decided, was that they had no intention of dropping the matter of Vincent Dawson. They just wanted her to believe she could be protected.

"Shall I look into the Federal Witness Protection Program?" the general asked.

"And advertise where she is?" Burt asked in disgust. "In all likelihood the man is going to be the president's assistant. We have to hide her ourselves. I'm thinking that I know the perfect place, but we'll talk about that later, Mac."

Sterling heard the emphasis on *later* and knew that this powerful group didn't even trust each other. There would be no inside information for her here. So long as her life was at risk, they weren't going to talk about their plans. Reluctantly, she allowed herself to seem to agree. Whatever she did, she'd have to do it alone.

"Thank you, all of you," she said. "But I'll figure out my own future."

Sterling signed off, sorry now that she'd been so quick to close and lock her door. If she were in a normal office, with normal windows and doors, she could simply crack open her door and listen. Her safe haven was definitely a prison.

Shangri-la not only kept the world out, it kept people in.

A short time later the locked door opened and Jessie came inside, pushing Sterling's wheelchair. "Mrs. Everett said for me to come and get you for lunch. I thought you didn't go anywhere without your chair."

"Normally I don't. But I've decided I need to practice. Lately, I've had to get where I wanted to go on my own."

"Speaking of going somewhere, I called you this morning to see if you wanted to have breakfast with me. Where were you?"

"I . . . I must have been in the shower," Sterling said, uncomfortable at breaking her vow of honesty to Jessie. But there were times when a little white lie was necessary.

Jessie glared at her doubtfully. "Uh-huh. Well, are you ready to go?"

"Sure. I'm starving."

Jessie held the chair while Sterling sat down, then flipped the footrests down.

"By the way, Jess, I'm curious. I thought I locked the door you just came in."

"You did, but if you know the code, you can override the computer. Don't tell Dad, okay?"

Sterling had the feeling that she hadn't fooled Jessie at all. Maybe her breakfast call had been in person. She'd spent most of her life at Shangri-la. She probably knew more about the computer security program than Mac thought.

That didn't make Sterling feel particularly good. Neither did Burt's broad grin when he brought their food. "Sorry you missed—breakfast, Sterling. I made you an extra-big salad for lunch. By now . . . you must really be hungry."

"Not more casserole?" she managed to say, more sweetly than he expected.

"Oh, no. I decided Mac was right. Casserole is off the menu. I've switched to seafood salad for you two."

"And what are you serving Mac—nails?"

Burt's grin widened. "Nah, I figure he needs a big batch of oysters."

When Burt left, Jessie picked up her fork, looked at Sterling, and said, "You ought to know that I approve of you and Mac. It will just take a little getting used to."

"Jessie, there is no me and Mac."

"Oh? Whatever you say. But I think there is. It'll be so good to have someone here that isn't old. We can watch movies, swim, do . . . girl things."

Sterling sat back with a sigh. "Jessie, you need someone your own age to do things with, and you need to do those things away from here, out in the real world. If you transferred to your college campus, you'd have so many new and exciting experiences out there."

Jessie's face went stark white. "No! I can't do that!"

"Why not? Your life isn't in danger, and whatever physical problems you had seem to have been solved. Trust me, Jessie, isolating yourself is wrong."

"I thought you understood. I never leave the

mountain." She stood. "It isn't that I don't want to. I can't!" With that, Jessie ran out of the room.

Sterling sat, staring down at her salad in dismay.

"Don't feel bad, Sterling." Burt interrupted. He had obviously been listening around the corner. "That's what she does when someone tries to get her away. The only thing that's worse is when Mac forces her."

"What happens then?"

"She has extreme anxiety attacks. Can't breathe, can't see, and finally she passes out. He's tried everything. Brought in the best doctors. Nothing works."

"But why? Why won't Jessie leave the mountain?"

"Because the only time she ever left was the time her mother died. Jessie still holds herself responsible for Alice's death. She wasn't responsible; the woman killed herself and she almost killed Jessie. Alice was so messed up by then that she thought it was the only way to save herself. Jessie was too young to understand her mother's problems, and how selfishly her mother acted."

"How awful. What about Mac? Is that why he rarely leaves?"

"Mac? No, Mac is doing penance. He was gone at the time of the accident. Alice begged him to stay, told him that she'd kill herself if he left. She'd threatened this so many times before that he didn't believe her."

"But this time she was serious."

"She was and it's hard to tell whether Mac or Jessie carries around the most guilt."

Sterling finished her lunch in silence, picking out the shrimp and leaving the rest untouched. What a group of wounded people they were. Mac and Jessie were prisoners of their past pain, hiding away in a mountain. She'd also hidden herself away in a prison. Now she was going to disappear, become another person in a new life where she'd be just as much a prisoner as she was before.

Back in her quarters, Sterling picked up the gift she discovered outside Mac's door, still wrapped in shiny paper and Christmas ribbons. More secrets, she thought as she ripped the foil away revealing a small box. Inside the box was a handmade, roughly crafted bell. A slip of paper enclosed explained that the bell was a replica of the one in the chapel by the lake at the foot of the mountain.

The legend of the bell explained that early Spanish travelers retreated to the mountain in time of trouble to ask for help. The people in the valley below knew when they heard the bells ring that their prayers had been answered.

An artist, recovering at Shangri-la from drug addiction, had sculpted the bell, ringing it triumphantly when he left. Mac had the piece reproduced and given to all who came to the mountain searching for refuge.

Sterling cradled the small rough piece of art in her hand. Would it ring for her?

Vincent Dawson sat at the bar and cradled his drink with one hand. He was waiting, waiting for the man who would erase all his problems. Downtown Washington in December was a lonely place. Congress had been adjourned. Most of the senators and representatives had taken their families home. But he'd come back alone. That move was rare, for he usually stayed at his boss's side. In order to make his return to the capital believable, he hinted that he had a new lady friend who lived there.

Much of the work he did for the senator had never been revealed. March was weak and easily led, but now and then a stubborn streak of decency, a result of his wife's rapidly eroding influence, asserted itself. He was confused and scared by the airport incident. Vincent explained that the search of the airport was brought on by a bomb scare, but that it had been nothing to worry about.

Having sat at the bar for over an hour, Vince decided that Jonah apparently wasn't coming.

He drained his glass, stood, and buttoned his overcoat before exiting into the wind and cold. As he walked toward his car a figure joined him.

"About time," the man said.

"Who are you?" Vincent asked, glancing around at the deserted street. He could be mugged or killed and nobody would know.

"Who'd you send for?"

"Jonah?"

"Let's not use names. Get in your car and tell me what you need."

That wasn't what Vincent had in mind. Talking in a bar was one thing. Driving off with a hit man was not the kind of risk he was prepared to take.

"Make up your mind. Either we go together, or I'm out of here."

Vince unlocked the car doors and crawled behind the wheel. Jonah waited until the lights in the car went off, then got inside.

"Drive."

Fourteen blocks later Vincent had explained his situation.

"Everybody knows about that mountain. It's a fortress. No one could get inside. Draw the woman out and I'll take care of her."

"How?"

"That's up to you. There's a chapel on the lake at the base of the mountain. Get her there. Once it's set up, call me at this number. It'll cost you fifty thousand dollars cash."

"Fifty thousand dollars? I don't have that much."

"Then you'd better get it. You've got three days."

"You'll be at this number?"

"No, but my answering machine will. Just say 'Rendezvous at midnight' and I'll know."

ELEVEN

For the next three days both Mac and Jessie avoided Sterling. Even Elizabeth seemed distant.

The only friendly face in the compound was Burt's and he constantly plied her with food, pretending that nothing was different.

"Sorry, Sterling, Mac doesn't cut me in on his plans unless I need to know," Burt told her one afternoon in her quarters.

"Would you tell me if he did?"

"No, probably not."

"I haven't seen much of Jessie," she said. "Is she—okay?"

"If you're asking if she's upset about you and Mac, I don't think so. Confused maybe. Even though she's happy for her father, sharing you with him is something she'll have to get used to."

"Burt, I'm not sharing Mac with anyone!"

"Good for you. He needs someone to give it to him but good."

"No, you don't understand. I'm leaving. I can't stay here. But I can't leave, not without his approval. I don't even know the way out."

"This isn't about leaving, this is about Mac," Burt said. "You won't let yourself care about Mac. Why? Are you afraid that he doesn't feel the same way about you?"

"I don't feel any way, Burt. Mac brought me here and he's completely taken over my life. I'll admit it would be easy to just let him, but I can't. I just can't."

Burt glanced at her, puzzled. "I was under the impression that you called Mac and *asked* for his help."

"Well—I did. But I didn't expect all—this."

"Sterling, most people turn to those they care about when trouble comes. Just like you did."

She looked at Burt, with all the sadness she felt apparent in her eyes. "Yes, but don't you see, Mac helps everyone. I'm just the latest of his projects."

"I don't think so," Burt protested. "And neither do you or Mac. You just don't know how to let go of the pain you've wrapped yourself in. That might hurt even more."

Long after Burt left, Sterling thought about what he said. Mac was no stranger to her. Granted, she'd never seen him before her arrival in New Orleans, but they'd talked so often, about so much. No, that wasn't true. They'd talked about the football player who couldn't face a future outside of sports and the young woman assigned to help him find another future to focus on. There was the librarian who lost her memory and the Gypsy doctor who helped restore it. And then Conner, who'd been separated from Erica by a lie that nearly cost them everything.

Now Mac had taken on Sterling Lindsey, whether she wanted it or not. Maybe if she knew she could leave, she wouldn't feel so trapped.

Sterling finally turned to her only link to escape, her computer. It was time she learned about Shangri-la.

After extensive searching, she found a topographical map of the mountain and the surrounding area, both before Mac's alterations and after.

Their arrival had been cloaked in darkness and Mac's window on the world didn't show the area directly beneath the steep cliffs. But the map revealed a large lake at the base, fed by the underground river in which she'd swum for her exercise.

Later that afternoon she explored the path of the water as a potential escape route. She managed to enter the hole in the rock through which the water disappeared, but it soon narrowed to several smaller openings, too small for her to get through.

Discouraged, she went back to the office, where she found the elevators that led to the top, but those going to the base of the fortress were in a different location. And she had no doubt that Mac had made the exit too difficult to use and hidden it so well that outsiders couldn't gain access to it.

Still, from the hushed tones of Mac's friends, she knew that Jonah was a feared man. If anyone could get to her, it would be Jonah. And if that happened, Mac and Jessie would be in danger. She couldn't let that happen. Not to two people she loved.

Love? Where had that come from? She was simply a friend to Jessie and a willing playmate in Mac's bed. There was no room for, nor any suggestion of, love or commitment. There couldn't be. The obstacles and the risks were too great.

Vincent Dawson might not be her biggest enemy, after all. She had to find a way to escape.

For hours she looked at the plans, thinking, studying, coming up with new ideas, and discarding them. Finally, she leaned back and closed her eyes. Vincent Dawson might not be able to get in, but it appeared equally unlikely that she would be able to get out. She started looking for Mac but couldn't find him anywhere.

She finally gave up and went to Jessie's room. "I hate to bother you, Jessie, but do you know where your father is?"

"I haven't been able to find him. I . . . I thought he was with you."

"I haven't seen him for several days."

"But you work in the office right next door and you two are . . ."

"We aren't anything, Jessie. You jumped to conclusions that were—wrong."

She looked puzzled. "But I thought . . . I mean

I know Mac is . . . interested in you. Anyone can see that."

"He only thought he was. At any rate, that's all over. But I do need to talk to him, and he seems to be avoiding me. Do you think you could find him?"

Jessie studied Sterling for a moment and said exactly what was on her mind. "Let me tell you something, Sterling. Whatever Mac does, he thinks it through and then he acts. If he didn't do that with you, it's because you hit him broadside when he wasn't expecting it." She grinned. "Imagine that, the big man got himself into something he couldn't handle and he ran."

"Jessie, I don't think it's quite like that. There are some things you don't know, things I'm not at liberty to tell."

"No problem, Sterling. He's always telling me to break out of this jail and get a life. It's time he had a little help practicing what he preaches." She picked up the phone. "Elizabeth, I'd like to speak to my father. Where is he?"

She listened a moment. "I don't believe that. You always know where he is." She punched another number on the phone. "Burt, where's my father?" Her expression was even more puzzled as she dialed yet a third time. "Joseph, tell my father that I have a problem and I need to speak to him immediately."

Finally, she replaced the handset and turned to Sterling. "I don't understand. Nobody seems to know where he is. Either he's left the mountain or he's refusing to talk to me."

"I can't believe he'd refuse to talk to you, Jessie. Is it possible that he has left? Would you know if he did?"

"No," she admitted, "not unless he told me. There are helicopters and planes coming and going around here all the time."

"What about cars? Does everyone fly in and out?"

"No. I think that some of the construction materials are trucked in. And food supplies. But the only way I've left the mountain—since the . . . accident . . . is by air."

Sterling knew how hard that statement was for Jessie to make. So far Jessie had never talked about the accident except to say her mother had been killed and she'd been hurt. Sterling wondered how much she remembered.

"Your accident occurred here?"

"Yes. My mother . . . lost control of the car going down the mountain. It shot over the edge and landed in the lake. I was thrown out. She drowned."

"Do you know where the automobiles are kept?"

Jessie frowned. "I must have known once. But not now. I can't remember. Maybe Mac closed off the way."

Back at her computer, Sterling searched the archives once more. Finally, just as her eyes were crossing with exhaustion, she found it. The underground garage. It wasn't at the base of the mountain as she might have expected. It was about halfway to the top. The way to the bottom was apparently hazardous and no longer used.

Sterling leaned back in her chair and closed her eyes. Complications. Complications. She could almost understand Alice. Though she could never know what drove the tormented woman to suicide, she knew Mac well enough to know that he'd done everything possible to help Alice. Just as he was helping her. And she, too, was trying to escape. Like Alice, her own simple world had become more complicated than she could face.

Then a voice came on her computer. "You have mail."

She sat up. "Mac?"

The message spelled itself out on the screen. *Sterling, I have Mr. McAllister. I think you know that it's you I want. A simple trade will save him. Come alone, to the chapel on the lake, at dawn.*

There was no name at the bottom.

Jonah. The man who was sent to kill her wasn't going to invade Shangri-la; he'd found a way to make her come to him. She glanced at her watch. It said twelve midnight. She estimated that she had five hours before dawn. In five hours she had to find the way out of the mountain and to the chapel. Mac couldn't be sacrificed for her. There was Jessie to think about.

Sterling had cheated death once. Now she had to face the possibility that she might not be that lucky the second time around.

Hastily, she composed a note to Conner. He

ought to be told that Dawson had Mac and knew what she was doing, in case she failed. Briefly, she explained the situation, typed the E-mail, and set the computer to send it at seven A.M. That way, if she managed to free Mac, he could head off Conner's armed response and avoid bloodshed.

Sterling printed out the map of the old garage and the exit down the mountain. From the schematic, she could see no way to reach it, but that was the only way she could escape unnoticed by Mac's "Big Brother" spying system.

First, she had to change into some kind of reasonable dress. A fleece running suit over a flannel T-shirt. Heavy socks and running shoes. She reached for her purse, then laughed at herself. A driver's license was the least of her needs right now. What she ought to have was a gun and a flashlight.

She had neither.

Two hours later her legs were burning with fire and she'd begun to stumble. She still hadn't found the way to the garage and she was running out of time. Desperate and weak, she returned to her quarters, let herself inside, and sank into her wheelchair.

"Where've you been?"

It was Jessie, wiping sleep from her eyes. Dried tear streaks lined her cheeks.

"I—I was looking for the garage."

"I tried to reach you. Mac's gone. You were gone. I thought . . ."

Sterling forced herself to stand once more and made her way to the bed. She opened her arms and felt Jessie crumple against her. "You thought we'd both abandoned you?"

"I didn't know what to think." Jessie sniffed. "To start with, I was just mad. Then I got scared."

"So am I."

Jessie cried for a moment, then hushed. "Why were you going to the garage? Nobody goes there anymore."

Sterling thought about lying, then decided that she needed Jessie's help if she were going to save her father. "Jessie, I want you to do something for me. Will you?"

"If I can."

"Your father is in danger. He's been kidnapped by a very sinister man. I—I have to get to the garage. I need a car to get down the mountain and I need it quick."

"Mac's in danger? Why?"

"I can't tell you. Just know that I'm responsible. I brought the danger here and I have to end it."

Jessie leaned back and wiped the corner of her eyes with the tail of her nightgown. "I'll call Burt."

"No! Trust me, Jessie. I can't take the chance that Burt will stop me from leaving."

"But what can you do?"

"I can save Mac. If you'll help me."

"All right. Let's go."

They started toward the corridor, but Sterling's pain was so great that she had to hold on to the door or else she'd fall.

"What's wrong?" Jessie asked.

"I can't walk any farther right now. My legs need a rest."

"Let me get your chair." She pushed the chair to Sterling and waited.

"Damn!" *It isn't fair. The bastard that did this to me is about to hurt Mac and I can't even get to him to stop it.*

"Sit down, Sterling. Do you have anything to take—for pain?"

She did, but she couldn't afford to be fuzzy-headed now. "No," she said through clenched teeth. The pain wasn't letting go even as she lowered herself into the chair. "Just get me to the garage."

Jessie hesitated. "I'm not sure I know the way. I was a little girl then. And Mama—Mama was so upset that night. It was dark and I was afraid."

Sterling could sense her fear. Jessie's hands tightened around her chair and her body stiffened in fright. Sterling spoke softly to her. "Jessie, listen to me. I know you can do it. You need to. You can help Mac."

"I couldn't help my mother."

"You were a little girl then. Now you're an adult."

She hesitated a long time, then said, "Sterling, I never told Mac, but I didn't want to go. She was acting weird and I was scared."

"Why did you go?"

"I thought if I got in the car with her, she wouldn't leave."

"Jessie, stop. Take a deep breath and listen. She

was sick. She didn't know what she was doing. It was an accident. People who know how to deal with those things couldn't save your mother. Neither could you. But you may be able to help me save your dad."

Jessie tried to stop shaking. She loosened her grip and relaxed her shoulders. Her distress was still evident, but she was making a valiant attempt to control herself. "All right. I'll try to find the way, but I'm not sure I remember. And if Burt or Raymond tracks us, we're never going to get there."

"But you know a way to override the system, don't you?"

"Only to unlock doors. I learned to do that before Elizabeth came and the nannies would lock me in my room."

Sterling shuddered. What kind of lonely life must this girl have led? "Tell you what, let's get to my computer and see what we can do."

That step seemed innocent enough and Jessie agreed. But forty-five minutes later they were forced to give up. Jessie dashed back to her quarters to dress and they started down. From the family elevator, they switched to one of a series of service elevators. Jessie studied the panel.

"I'm not sure which floor it's on."

"If I read the plans right," Sterling said, "it's on the west side of the third level."

Jessie caught Sterling's shoulders and squeezed. "Let's do it."

The car descended, then came to a stop and the

door opened. The corridor beyond was dark and damp. There were no lights here. "Now what?" Jessie asked. "We could run right past the door and not know it."

Sterling allowed herself a small sigh. Her back hurt. Her legs hurt. Her heart hurt. What was Jonah doing to Mac? Would she be able to get there in time?

"Why does this man want you, Sterling?" Jessie asked.

"It's not important."

"Damn it, Sterling! I'm not a child. I'm twenty years old and I'm tired of everyone treating me like one."

"You're right, Jessie. If you're expected to be an adult, you should be given the respect due you. The man who has your father was hired by the man who shot me."

"Whoa! Why don't you just call the police?"

"Because he's a very important man in Washington. They wouldn't believe me and he'd win."

"And Mac knows the truth. That's why he brought you here—so the bad guys couldn't get you."

"Yes."

"Then what?"

Sterling didn't know how to answer her. "That's a good question. I guess we never got that far."

"So, since they couldn't get to you, they got to Mac, knowing you'd come to his rescue."

"Yes."

She started pushing Sterling down the dark corridor. "The question is, how'd they know?"

That caught Sterling by surprise. "What do you mean, how'd they know?"

"Well, if I knew that I'd die if I left here, I'd stay. How could they be certain that you'd come out to save my father?"

The blackness surrounded them. Sterling felt along the wall at intervals in order to keep from running into it in the darkness as she thought about Jessie's question. She was right. How could they be sure?

"Because," Jessie said, answering her own question, "somebody on the inside told them that you and Mac are in love. That's the only answer."

"But that's crazy. We're not. I mean . . . he's not. Your father and I met in person for the first time the day I came to New Orleans."

"But it's obvious that he cares. He seems younger, more carefree. I thought that you went way back."

"Well," Sterling considered, "I guess you could say we do. We've talked on the phone and through E-mail for years, ever since I started to work for Conner."

"Now Uncle Conner has Erica and you have Mac. At least you will once we outsmart the bad guys. I used to wish Uncle Conner was my dad. He seemed so cool, always had time to play with me."

"Your father loves you, Jessie. He just doesn't know how to deal with you as an adult."

"No. He tries but he's never known what to do with me."

In that moment Sterling knew that Jessie was wise beyond her years. And maybe she was right. Sterling hoped that Jessie was wrong about a spy inside reporting on their activities. Then, in the distance, they caught sight of a red light.

An exit sign.

Jessie let out a deep breath. "I think we found it, Sterling."

"I think you're right."

Jessie let go of the handles of the chair and walked to the door, running her fingertips up and down the frame and across the metal expanse. "There's no knob. No way to open it."

"The computer identifies your voice, doesn't it?" Sterling asked.

"Sure, and yours too."

"But I'm guessing that this is part of the old system. Let's see. Open." Nothing happened. "You try it."

Jessie took a deep breath in the silence. "Open! Open, you dumb, freaking door!"

"Jessie!"

"Oops, sorry. This is Jessie McAllister. Open!"

There was a rusty creak, the sound of metal against metal, and the door slid open.

"We did it! Sterling, we did it."

"Yes, we're somewhere. Can you find a light switch?"

"This is Jessie McAllister. Lights on!"

The lights responded, revealing a large room filled with what looked like road equipment, trucks, and . . . "A car," Sterling said, almost reverently. "Thank you, Jessie. I'll take it from here."

"Take it from where? I'm coming with you."

"No way. Your father's life is at stake. I'm not about to put you in danger."

"And you're going to drive?"

"Drive? Of course I am. I know how to drive." But could she? Conner provided a driver for her on the rare occasions when she left her apartment or the office. She hadn't tried to drive since she'd been shot. And she wasn't certain that her muscles would work fast enough to operate the brake and the gas pedal. Still, she had no choice.

"Sterling, the drive down the mountain is dangerous in the daytime. It's still dark out there and you aren't operating at full steam. Get in the car. I'll drive."

"And how much experience have you had, driving a car?"

"Just because I don't go anywhere doesn't mean I can't. I'll have you know it's sixteen miles around the perimeter of the airfield. At one end there's even a space to parallel park. I may not know the road, but I can handle the car. Just call me Mario Andretti."

Sterling wanted to argue with Jessie, but she was losing time. Mac's life was at stake. "All right. But when we get almost there, I want you to drop me off, turn the car around, and go back inside the mountain."

Jessie didn't answer. Instead, she pushed Sterling to the passenger side of a Blazer, opened the door, and waited.

Sterling forced herself to her feet. She couldn't hold back a moan. She had no choice. Jessie would have to drive. "So, how do we get out of the building?"

She closed the door behind Sterling then moved to the driver's side. Reaching for the switch, her fingertips hit and jingled the keys. "Well, I suppose we could crash through like they do in one of those action movies. On the other hand, maybe there's a garage-door opener."

There wasn't.

But when she turned on the lights in the vehicle, she saw the computer built into the console. "What do you think?"

Sterling studied the piece of equipment. "Turn on the switch." As soon as Jessie did, the engine caught and the lights came on. After a few mistakes Sterling punched in the right combination, and like the window on the world in Mac's office, the wall opened.

"All right, Jessie. Let's go."

Jessie drove through the opening and stopped. Sterling waited, assuming that she was studying the road that wound around the rocks and disappeared from sight. But she didn't move. The darkness above was growing faintly lighter.

"We have to go, Jessie. It's almost dawn."

"I—I'm trying."

Sterling turned. Even in the darkness she could see Jessie's hands clutching the wheel. The sound of her breath was growing shallower and faster.

"Jessie! You can do this. I know you can. Mac is down there and he needs us."

"I thought I could, but I can't. Don't you understand. I can't leave. I'll die."

Sterling had to think quickly and divert Jessie's attention so that she could somehow gain Jessie's trust and confidence. "Jessie. I haven't been entirely honest with you. I'm in love with your father. Because I love him, I can do this. Because you love him, too, you can help me. Do you understand?"

The breathing became rougher.

"You aren't responsible for what happened to your mother."

"I should—have—stopped her."

"You couldn't have. I may not be able to save Mac, but I'm going to try and you have to help me. We can do this, together. Jessie, drive!"

Slowly, an inch at a time, the vehicle moved forward.

"That's it, a little faster," Sterling encouraged.

They rounded the big rocks and the enormity of what she was asking came clear. The drive curved around the mountain, narrow, winding. Sterling didn't need sunlight to know that the drop-off on her side plunged, sheer and vertical, straight into nothingness.

"I'm going to swap myself for your father," Sterling said, trying to keep her voice calm when she was almost as scared as Jessie. "The kidnapper has no use for Mac. I'm the one he wants. Then I'll explain that I can't identify the killer. He was wearing a mask. I never really saw his face."

"You think he'll believe you?"

Sterling didn't know, but it was the only chance Mac had. "Of course," she said confidently.

They moved slowly down the mountain. Sterling spoke to Jessie as if she were addressing the five year old child that she was when her mother had driven the car wildly down this same road.

Sterling glanced at her watch and back at the sky. It was almost daybreak, dawn, the appointed hour. Then the lake came into view, a smear of dark against the sky.

"We're almost there, Jessie. Look, there's the chapel. When we reach it, I want you to turn around and drive back. Alert Burt and Joseph."

Jessie still didn't speak, but color seemed to be returning to her knuckles.

"There, in the churchyard, there's enough room for you to let me out and turn around."

"No," Jessie finally said, in a low whisper. "I won't leave you. I won't let you die too."

Then they'd reached the chapel. The sun lightened the sky enough that Sterling could see there were no other cars. There was only a dock and maybe a boat at the end of it.

Jessie stopped. Sterling took a deep breath and opened the door. Jessie started to get out.

"Drive away, Jessie. Let them think that you've gone."

"What good will that do? This man will know that someone else knows what's going on."

"I'm guessing that he expected that and has made plans. Just go far enough that he'll think you've left."

"I am not letting you go down there alone."

"Please, Jessie. We don't know what to expect. You may have to drive your father away. Please, Jessie. I need you to do this."

"All right," she whispered. "But I'll wait just around those rocks—for now."

Sterling got out of the car, cursing her weak legs, determined to walk as far as she had to in order to save Mac. The area around the chapel was paved, and the door was wide open. She walked in slowly, fighting the pain pulsing in her legs. A dim light beckoned from within.

Candles behind the altar were burning. But there was no one inside.

TWELVE

"Mac?"

Sterling's voice echoed through the chapel, bouncing off the walls and fading into the distance.

She took several steps into the church, listening, waiting, then stopped and took a deep breath. The pain in her legs now stretched from her knees to her neck, intensifying with every move. Pain was nothing new. Of late, she'd taken the easy way out and not forced herself to walk. Now pain became a welcome reminder that she was alive and ready for her mission.

There was no point in being subtle. She had come to exchange herself for Mac and that was what she had to do.

"Mac? Are you here?"

But she didn't have to go any farther to know that she was alone. Where was Jonah? There was no one in the church. But, obviously someone had been there. Someone had lit candles that barely brought any light to the room. Where was he?

She tried calling again "Jonah? Show yourself. I came alone, unarmed." She held up her arms. "Surely you're not afraid of a woman."

Nothing.

A heavy sensation settled in her stomach. Suppose she'd made a mistake in coming? Where was Mac? And how long would Jessie remain quietly in the truck before chasing after her?

Sterling turned and made her way back to the courtyard. The moon had set, the sunrise casting faint shimmerings of light against the horizon. Beyond the chapel the lake was becoming clearer. She could see it now and hear the water lapping against the stony shore. How did he get here, this Jonah who killed people for money?

If he'd come by car, someone would have known. A plane was out of the question. Boat. He must have come across the lake. Sterling started toward the water, saying a silent prayer that Jessie would stay put.

Then she saw it, at the end of the dock, a pale ghost of an object, undulating in the water. Jonah had arrived in a speedboat. Past a tall evergreen tree that had found enough soil to put down roots, she moved forward, pausing at every other plank in the dock to listen. There was nothing but the sound of the boat knocking a piling.

From across the water a bird called out, its eerie cry sending prickles up her spine. The wind swept across the water and caught her hair, ruffling it across her face. She drew in an icy breath and shivered.

"Jonah? I've done what you wanted. Now show yourself."

There was a muffled sound and a thump.

Why hadn't he just told her to come to the dock? Because by doing it this way, he could see whether or not she was by herself.

Then a large shadow slipped out of the darkness. "Good of you to come, Ms. Lindsey." The voice was slightly foreign, with no characteristics distinct enough to identify the country. "But you didn't come alone. Someone came with you."

"Yes. I couldn't drive down the mountain. You see, I'm usually in a wheelchair. I had to have someone drive me because my legs aren't that strong or reliable. Don't worry. She won't interfere."

"Oh, I'm not worried. Mac is my guarantee that nobody will interfere."

Sterling's heart hammered in her throat.

"Where's Mr. McAllister?"

The muffled sound continued and her shadowman laughed. "Let's just say he's tied up at the moment. Come closer."

"Not until I see Mac. Where is he?"

"In the boat."

"Let me see Mac." She swallowed her fear and moved forward. "Step aside, please."

As she moved closer she saw that Jonah was a black man, a large black man with handsome features and a bald head.

"I must say, I'm surprised at how easy you're making this," another voice said as a second man came out of the cabin. "I wasn't certain you would."

"I was told to come," she said in surprise. "Now let Mac go."

"I don't think so, babe. You got in the way. Now you've got to be dealt with."

"You're going to kill us both, aren't you?"

"Technically, Jonah will do it. But the end result is the same."

"But you don't understand. That's why I came. I can't identify you or anyone else. I've already been through this with the police. They actually thought I was your accomplice. They didn't believe me before, they certainly won't believe me now. So you can just let us both go."

"I don't think so."

She was getting frantic. She hadn't planned on Vince being here. She and Mac might be able to handle one man, but not two. "How can you be certain I'm really alone? There might be ten men in the back of the Blazer."

"But those ten men don't want Mr. McAllister to die, do they? And if Jonah doesn't get back into the boat and reset the timer, a bomb will go off in approximately five minutes."

"What do you intend to blow up?" she asked, trying to peer past the man blocking her view.

"I believe it's called Shangri-la?"

"No! You can't. You told me to come. I did. No one other than my driver knows what you're doing.

For God's sake, Mr. Dawson, you've got what you want, I'm here. Let Mac go." She walked toward him.

"So you do know me."

"I didn't know ten years ago, but I know now."

"And you can walk . You're recovered."

"Not really. Your bullet saw to that. If you want me to come closer, someone will have to help me. I can't get myself into that boat alone. My legs are growing weaker by the minute."

"Do it," Dawson ordered.

Jonah stepped into the boat, reached out, and lifted Sterling inside. With the added weight, the craft dipped dangerously and Jonah staggered, almost dropping Sterling. As she grabbed him she felt something stuck in his belt. A knife. Faking a stumble, she pulled it from beneath his shirt and slid it up her sleeve.

"Be still, woman!" he growled, his eyes wide with something almost like fear. He was afraid. Of what? Certainly not her. The boat? No. The water! Yes, that was it . . . Jonah was afraid of the water. Vincent might have devised the plan to lure her out and take her across the lake because it was the only chance he had, but she was beginning to believe that perhaps Jonah couldn't swim.

Finally, he deposited her on the middle seat. Then she saw Mac. He was tied up on the front seat, tape plastered across his mouth. Something wasn't right. He was too still.

"What have you done to him." She started toward Mac.

"Stay put, lady," Jonah snapped as he moved to the back of the craft where the engine was clamped on.

"He's just a little sleepy," Dawson said. "You see, he got up earlier than you did."

"All right," she said to her captors. "You have me. Let him go."

Vince laughed. "Not yet. You might not have alerted the others to your mission, but I don't think I'll take any chances."

"Are you going to disconnect the timer on the bomb now?" she asked.

"Not just yet. Maybe when we get to the middle of the lake. I wouldn't want you to jump overboard."

Sterling's mind went to fast forward. What on earth was she going to do? She could see Mac's eyes now. Though his body gave every indication that he was drugged, his eyes were frantically blinking. A quick glance at Jonah's grim expression told her that he was as ready to get this settled as she was. They just had different ideas about the outcome.

Neither Jonah nor Dawson was wearing a life jacket.

She didn't doubt that they'd planted a bomb, maybe more than one, somewhere in the rocks at the base of the mountain. If she didn't find a way to stop them, everyone inside would be killed. The sanctuary would be destroyed.

She'd brought all this terror to Shangri-la. She'd

put the man she loved at risk and he'd never know how she felt. "Mac," she said, "there's something I need to tell you."

"Don't move!" Dawson barked.

The engine started with a roar, and the boat backed slowly around, then shot forward. Sterling guessed that by now they had less than a minute left before the bomb would explode. She didn't fool herself. Vince had already killed one man. He wasn't going to let Mac go. And the lake would make a lovely place for a drowning. Was that the plan?

"Mr. Dawson," she said hesitantly. "I've done just what you asked. Nobody is chasing you and I'm willing to go with you. Will you do something for me?"

"What?"

"Let me remove Mac's gag. What harm can it do? I know you're going to kill us and I'd like to kiss him good-bye."

"So, my contact was right. There is something going on between you. Personally, I didn't believe the great Lincoln McAllister would go for a woman physically handicapped like you, but different strokes for different folks."

"I know. It came as a surprise to me too. But I love him and he loves me. Surely there's someone, somewhere, you care about. What harm can it do? He's in no condition to do anything."

Mac's eyes closed and he moaned.

"Please?" she asked again.

"Why not? Do it, Jonah," Dawson ordered, and

took the wheel. Jonah glanced at his watch, then moved quickly toward Mac, stripping the tape from his mouth.

"I'm sorry, Mac," Sterling said, "but I'm not going to die without you knowing how I feel." She stood. "I love you, darling." She stumbled, rocking the boat.

Jonah panicked and reached for Sterling. "You aren't going to turn us over, lady. Drowning me ain't part of the plan. I only got half the money now. You ain't gonna cheat me out of the rest. Not as long as I have this little device in my hand."

"Forget about her! Set off the charge, Jonah," Dawson yelled. "Here's as good a place as any."

"Jump, Sterling!" Mac suddenly said in a low, controlled voice.

She stumbled, and her weight combined with Mac's tilted one side of the boat dangerously. "Good idea," she agreed, and pushed Mac overboard, jumping in behind him.

The water was like ice and as black as night. With Mac's feet and hands tied, he couldn't swim. It was up to her to save him.

"Mac?"

"Over here," he sputtered.

Both she and Mac went under as the pressure of the water slammed against them. The rope around his wrists was tight but thin. She sawed frantically with the stolen knife, felt one rope snap, then the other. Mac began to move his arms, propelling them to the surface.

Sterling sucked in a breath of air, then dived back into the water, cutting the ropes from his feet. Pain shot through her as the cold turned her limbs numb, forcing her to move slower and slower.

"Mac, get on your back and relax." As she started toward shore she heard a scream of terror. "Let go of me, man!"

Only a few yards away, the boat began to rock. "Give me the control," Dawson was yelling.

"No way, man. You'll just push me overboard and I'll die out here."

"You're going to die anyway," Dawson yelled, grabbing for the little black device. The struggle ended abruptly when Jonah plunged into the water, flinging the control unit over his shoulder as he fell.

Sterling began to swim frantically, tugging at Mac as she tried to move them away. She expected any second to be caught up in the blast of the explosion. But it didn't happen.

Without the control box, Dawson couldn't detonate the bomb. He revved the engine, made a circle, and turned the boat. Though he was having difficulty piloting the craft, he had one goal in mind and was going to finish things once and for all. They were going to be run down.

Then she heard the sound of another boat approaching from the rear.

"Hold on, Sterling!" The second boat flew past them, heading directly for Dawson. In it were Conner and Burt.

By the time Dawson realized what was happening, it was too late. Conner's boat plowed into the front of Dawson's boat, sent it into a spin, and hit it again in the rear. There was a gunshot and an explosion that caused a huge wave of water to crash over Sterling and Mac. Mac went under. Sterling caught hold of him and kicked frantically, ignoring the pain in her legs as she moved.

Moments later Conner had turned and directed his sputtering craft back to where Sterling had grabbed a piece of the wreckage and draped Mac across it. Her legs had stopped hurting. They were now completely numb.

Conner's boat reached them and came to a stop. "Need a ride?"

"Conner, get Mac. He's been drugged."

"Sure thing," he said, and reached for Mac. "What about it, buddy, did our plan work, or what?"

"I think it's more like 'or what,'" Mac whispered, then closed his eyes and went limp. They caught him as he slid back into the water, then pulled him into the boat. Moments later Sterling had joined him and was being covered with blankets and plied with hot coffee.

"Drink this," Burt instructed.

"Not now. How's Mac?"

"Half-frozen, but we're ready to warm him up. We've already called the Angel Ambulance Service. Drink!"

She took a sip, not even feeling the hot liquid as she swallowed it. Burt was wrapping Mac in warm blankets and massaging his hands while Conner coaxed his damaged boat back to shore.

"Want to tell me how you got here so fast?" she finally asked.

"We'd have come sooner if it hadn't been for the bomb."

"How'd you know about it?"

"Mac was wired. We were trying to create a diversion. Then it didn't matter. Jonah lost the triggering device."

"Are you telling me that you knew all about Mac being a prisoner?"

"Yep. And we knew about your little trip to the garage. We were onto it from the time you got Vince's message."

"You could have made it a little easier."

"We did. We turned on the exit light so you could find the door and made sure you had a vehicle to drive."

"Why didn't you say something?"

"We figured the only reason he had to bring you to the chapel was because he intended to go by boat. We weren't going to let anything happen to you."

"So you let them drug Mac. Didn't it occur to you that we might drown? Shades of the *Titanic*."

"Well, that wasn't part of the plan. We were all set to storm the Bastille when Dawson mentioned the bomb in the boat. Then we had to drop back and punt. Good thing you had a plan. What did you expect to do if we hadn't been waiting in the wings?"

"Sign up for Danish lessons in heaven, I guess."

Conner gave her a hard look. "Do what?"

"Don't ask. Just get us to one of Mac's medical specialists."

"Aye-aye, Captain. They're waiting for both of you."

"Where's Jessie?"

"Now, that's the strangest thing of all. We relayed our conversations through the computer in the Blazer. Once she knew the two of you were safe, she drove herself straight back up the mountain. Last I heard she was rapping at the top of her lungs along with Puff Daddy."

"Good for her. She did what she had to do. She couldn't save her mother, but she saved her father. Maybe Jessie will be okay now."

They reached the shore and Sterling watched as two paramedics transferred Mac into the back of a van. They started to close the doors when one of them stopped and called out, "Ms. Lindsey?"

"Yes?"

"He wants you to ride inside the van. Are you up to it?"

She was.

Conner helped her inside.

"Jessie's all right," he said. "Mac's gonna be all right. What about you, Sterling?"

"Don't worry about me, Conner. I'll find out and let you know."

She sat down on a bench beside the gurney where Mac was lying. The doors closed and the van moved off.

"Sterling?"

"I'm here."

"You're too far away. Come closer."

His voice was low and thready. She could barely hear him. Only when he flexed his fingers and motioned to her did she slide down the bench beside his head. She looked at him, so still and cold, and fought for words. But she couldn't find them.

"Closer," he repeated.

She leaned over him so that he could see her.

"About that speech . . ."

"Speech?"

"In the boat. About telling me you love me . . ."

"Don't worry, Mac. I was just making it up, stalling for time. I thought if I could get us into the water, I might be able to get you to shore. But I didn't know whether or not you could breathe. And I had to be able to find you."

He coughed, a watery, rattling cough, and turned his head toward her. "You probably could have saved yourself, Sterling. But without you, I'd have died."

"Hush now. You're too weak to talk. Just be quiet."

"All right. You talk. Tell me again."

"Tell you what?"

"About loving me."

She'd known from the moment they were pulled into the boat that she'd have to deal with what she'd said. But she hadn't expected it to happen quite so soon. What could she say?

"Later, Mac. After the doctors check you."

"Promise?"

"I promise."

"Who was the mole?" Sterling asked Burt.

"What mole?"

"Someone on the inside kept Vince informed. He knew about Mac and me, enough to know that I'd come."

"Oh, that mole. That was one of my men. I bring in people now and then, for rehabilitation."

"You mean to save them from the mob."

"Well, let's just say that I still have friends in low places who like our little hideout enough to stay and do small favors in return. He was more than happy to pass on what I told him. Now quit worrying."

Sterling wasn't worrying, she was bored and ready to get out of the hospital bed she'd been assigned to. Her little dip in the New Mexican mountain lake had done no damage. But the doctors had X-rayed, poked, prodded, and examined. The MRI she'd undergone this morning was the last straw.

"Burt, tomorrow's Christmas Eve, and if you don't get me out of here by dinnertime, I'll personally build a bomb and blow the place up."

Burt chuckled.

"I didn't miss seeing what happened out there, did I? The boat did blow up, didn't it?"

He nodded. "The boat did blow up. The gas tank exploded on impact."

"And Vincent Dawson and Jonah?"

"Take a look. It's very sad." He handed her a newspaper.

Inch-high headlines read: DEAD IN FISHING ACCIDENT IN NEW MEXICO—VINCENT DAWSON. INFLUENTIAL WASHINGTONIAN AND AIDE TO PRESIDENTIAL HOPEFUL DIES IN BOATING ACCIDENT OVER CHRISTMAS VACATION.

The story went on to explain that both Dawson and a companion were fishing when their boat capsized due to an explosion from a faulty fuel line. Neither man left behind any family. Senator March was in seclusion; his office issued a statement that the holiday this year would be very sad.

"He's really dead?" she asked.

"He's really dead. Now, Mac has been asking for you. He's been giving his doctors hell because they won't let him out of bed. I thought I might smuggle you in."

"Forget it, Burt," Mac said from the hallway. Moments later a wheelchair rolled in, bumping one doorway and then the other. "Go find Elizabeth and Jessie and get started putting up the tree. It's Christmas."

"Elizabeth said I wasn't to leave you."

"You're already henpecked, Burt. Get out of here."

"All right, if you're sure. What about it, Sterling?" Burt stood beside her bed, grinning from ear to ear. "I could always prepare another casserole."

"You've already done enough cooking," she said.

Burt planted a kiss on her forehead, gave Mac a jaunty little salute, and left the room.

"Close door," Mac commanded. "And lock!"

He wheeled his chair as close to Sterling's hospital bed as he could, leaned down, raised the footrests, and stood.

"Damn! If your legs hurt as bad as my feet, I don't know how you ever got away from that bastard in the airport."

"What are you doing, Mac?"

"I'm coming in for a bedtime story. Move over."

She pulled back the sheet and slid as far as possible to the side.

Mac unfastened the ties to his robe, let it fall to the floor, and there he stood, totally, gloriously nude.

"Mac, do the doctors know where you are?"

"Probably everybody on the mountain knows where I am, Sterling. And you know what?"

"What?"

"I don't care."

"Lights dim!" Sterling said.

"Sorry, darling, your voice patterns aren't programmed into the hospital yet. But you have the right idea. Lights dim!"

The room grew dark.

Seconds later the merry sounds of Christmas jingled through the intercom. "You better watch out—"

"Cancel that order," Mac barked. "Lights out."

An hour passed before he and Sterling settled

into each other's arms, sated and dreamy. "When I think how close I came to losing you," Mac said.

"And I you. How did they get you, Mac? Vincent and Jonah?"

"I made it easy for them. When they sent you the first message, Conner and I made our plan."

"What first message? The only one I saw was the one that said they'd captured you."

"There was another, one that said they had captured Erica. They'd only let her go if I gave them you."

"On, no! Is Erica all right?"

"She was always safe. They just disabled her telephone and computer so that she had no contact with the outside world. As soon as the phone went, she moved to a secure place. The men who'd disabled her equipment were captured and held. Let's just say they weren't happy when it was me instead of you on the first trip."

Sterling tried not to notice what he was doing with his hands. "What made you think you could fool them?"

"I never thought I would. But I thought I could buy Jonah off. I didn't count on Vince coming along."

"Doesn't make any sense that he was."

"He was paranoid. The only way he could be certain that you were really dead this time was to see it. When I turned up, he had to devise another plan."

"But didn't he think that some of your men would stop him?"

"I'm afraid he overestimated my importance. He actually thought that they'd send you out to free me. But you, my dear Moneypenny, made your own plan. It was truly heartwarming to know how you really feel about me. One woman took her life to punish me and here you come, Miss Red-White-and-Blue, true to her man, ready to give her life to save mine."

He kissed her, tenderly and completely, erasing the sharp rebuke she'd been about to make.

Instead, she settled for "Ummm. Yes."

Much later he continued. "Once you recover from your surgery, we're going to take Jessie to school and then we're going on a long honeymoon. There are so many places I want to show you."

"Hmm . . . Wait a minute. What surgery?"

"The doctors think they can remove the bullet, Sterling. There's a new technique we've been experimenting with here in the research center. They won't promise that you'll ever be able to climb Mount Everest, but they believe they can stop the pain."

"Mac, you're a dear, sweet man, but no. I know you think you have to make everything right. But you can stop that now. My life is perfectly fine just like it is."

"Dear? Sweet? Remember who you're talking to. This is 007 and any secret agent worth his salt is sexy and dangerous."

"It's more than that, Mac. Don't you see. You're confused. You couldn't help Alice and you've spent your life making up for that."

"That's absolutely true," he agreed. "And I'm going to keep right on running Shangri-la. But you and I, we're right together. And I'm not going to let you go. If you want to live somewhere else, we will. Just don't be afraid, I'll be here with you—all the way."

"It isn't that, Mac. It's just that I never expected to live a normal life. I've come to terms with my handicap and the life I live. I don't think I can chase a dream and fail. I couldn't survive that again."

"Why not?"

"Because I had that kind of dream once. Dreams don't last. You can't count on anything but yourself. This has been special, Mac, but I'm leaving—this afternoon if possible. Will you tell Conner to wait for me?"

"Conner went back last night."

Mac nuzzled her face, turning it up so that he could kiss her. "Sterling, I'm sorry, but I'm pulling rank. You aren't leaving Shangri-la until I say so. And that isn't going to happen today."

The lights suddenly came on.

The music began once more.

And the door opened.

Mrs. Everett strode in. "Mr. McAllister, there's a phone call for you."

"There is nobody I want to talk to bad enough

for you to interrupt. How the hell did you get in here anyway?"

"Mr. McAllister, I can go anywhere in the mountain I want to go." She picked up the robe he'd discarded and laid it on the bed. "And I'll give you about two minutes to get your bare bottom covered and into this chair."

She turned her back and began tapping her foot.

Sterling giggled.

Mac swore.

"You're down to one," she said. "And your caller is waiting."

"All right. I'm coming."

He slid his feet over the edge of the bed, touched the floor, and swore again. As if he were walking on hot coals, Mac groaned and cursed while he put on the robe and sat down.

"This better be worth it, Elizabeth."

"It absolutely is," she said, giving Sterling a wink as she swung him around and headed through the door.

The call was from Conner.

"How are you?"

"You interrupted—what I was doing for this?"

"Yep and because I thought you and I'd better have a little talk."

"About what?" Mac barked.

"About Sterling and your intentions. She has no family, so that just leaves me."

"My intentions are to hang up this phone and get back to what I was doing before you called."

"Hold on, Mac. Be serious. Sterling is important to me. You have never been serious about a woman before. Are you now?"

Mac started to drop the phone, then stopped. Conner deserved an answer. "You're right," he said. "After I married Alice I tried to be what she needed. But no matter what I did, she was never happy."

"I know. And I know what it is to lose someone. When my brother died, I went a little crazy. You brought me to Shangri-la and turned your doctors loose on me. It worked."

"But it didn't work for Alice. I couldn't keep her safe. She killed herself and she almost killed Jessie. I thought I'd never get over that, until Sterling came along."

Conner's voice remained compassionate. "If you mean that, Sterling is the one you ought to be telling, not me."

"I intend to. When she came down that dock, I thought I would die. Then she saved my life, and because of her, Jessie is going away to school. I can't imagine life without Sterling. She's validated everything I've done. Without her, there is nothing."

"That's all I wanted to hear," Conner said. "She needs you, Mac, but you're going to have to convince her."

"Any suggestions?" Mac asked.

"Nope. You're on your own. Send me an invitation to the wedding."

Sterling didn't leave the compound. Instead, the next day, she found herself drinking hot cider and wondering where Mac was as she watched Jessie, Elizabeth, and Burt put the decorations on the new Christmas tree they'd set up in the family room.

Nobody mentioned Mac, and Sterling spent an hour biting her tongue to keep from asking where he was. Finally, with all the lights and decorations in place, the star was added to the top of the tree.

"What, no angel?" Sterling quipped.

"Mac's orders," Burt replied. "He's the head angel around here. Even if he did stand us up."

"Yeah, where is he?" Jessie asked, allowing disappointment to creep into her voice.

Burt took the light cord and held it up. "Just be patient. All things come to he or she who waits. Lights off!" Once it was dark, he plugged in the Christmas tree lights.

A chorus of ahhs filled the silence, interrupted by the sound of sleigh bells. The holographic wall came on and a picture of the rooftop and the starlit sky came into view. In the distance, from behind the mountain, a light moved through the sky, closer and closer, until it landed.

A sleigh, pulled by snorting reindeer, rolled into view and Santa, sporting a red suit, white hair and whiskers, and a fur-trimmed hat waved and got out.

"Ho! Ho! Ho!"

"I'm not believing this," Jessie said. "Santa Claus?"

The figure lifted his bagful of packages and walked out of the picture.

Sterling studied his awkward gait. Where had Mac found a picture that moved, a man who— "Mac?"

The door suddenly opened and Santa came inside. "Ho! Ho! Ho! I've got my list here and I'm checking it twice."

"Daddy!" Jessie moved into her father's arms, laughing and crying. "I can't believe you did this."

"Believe it, Jessie," he said, holding her close, his eyes closed. "Why shouldn't Santa come and bring special gifts to the people he loves most?"

Sterling felt a lump in her throat. How could she ever leave this man and these people? It would rip her heart out. For one brief moment, when Mac had explained about the surgery, she'd allowed herself to believe. But normal lives were for other women. She had her world, back in Virginia. It was the only one she dared trust.

For most of the day she'd gone back and forth about leaving. True, she could operate Paradox, Inc. from here. She'd proved that. True, the doctors might be able to help her pain, but she'd never be the kind of person Mac needed. He thought that he could make everything right, but suppose he couldn't. She didn't want to think about having to rebuild her world again. She couldn't take the chance.

Vincent Dawson was dead. Conner was with Erica. Jessie had just called her father "daddy," and Burt had his arm possessively around Elizabeth, whose eyes were moist with tears.

And Mac. Mac shoved his hat back and focused his eyes directly on Sterling. Finally he said, "I have gifts, but the most important gifts of all have already been given. New lives, for all of us. Jessie is going away to school. Elizabeth and Burt are going to be married. Sterling is free of the past."

"And," he went on, "so am I."

Burt cleared his throat. "So, boss, what's in the bag?"

Mac smiled. "Presents. Everyone, find a place and sit."

With great flourish, Mac drew the presents from his bag and presented them. "For Burt." He handed the man his gift and waited.

"Do I have to open it now?"

"Of course," Elizabeth insisted. "We all want to see."

When he peeled back the paper and revealed a nightshirt and matching cap, everyone laughed.

"Not from Victoria's Secret, but serviceable," Elizabeth said.

Her laughter died when she opened her gift and found out that it was a sexy garment straight out of the latest catalog. "I'm not holding this up," she sputtered. "I'm not even going to wear it."

Burt's face spread into a wide grin. "No? You're right, at least not for very long."

"Burt!" Elizabeth scolded. "Not in front of the child."

Jessie tore into her tiny box. "What child?" She opened the box to reveal a key. Lifting her eyes in question, she held it up. "A key?"

"To your new sports car, Jessie. A great-looking woman like you should have her own wheels. They represent your newly found freedom and self-confidence." He leaned over and kissed her. "You deserve the world, Jessie."

Jessie didn't even try not to cry. After wiping away the torrent of tears running down her face, she asked, "What about Sterling?"

Mac walked toward Sterling, handing her the last gift. "For the woman I love," he said dramatically, "the woman who is going to be the mother of my second child."

She couldn't speak. What could she have said? I don't love you. I'm not going to have your child? I . . . She peeled back the paper and opened her box. Inside was another box, a tiny one, which was empty.

"There's nothing there," she said.

"What would you like to be there, Sterling? If you could have anything in the world, what would it be?"

And then she knew. What she wanted was what she'd always wanted, to have someone love her. The career she could manage. Living without pain—well, she'd lived with it so long, she wouldn't know how to manage without it. Her apartment? An apartment was just furniture.

Finally she looked up. Everyone was watching. There was a hush in the room.

She stood, wincing but using the pain to remind her that she was truly alive. "You, Mac. I just want you."

He pulled off his hat and the long white beard. Then he took a step forward, pulled her into his arms, and kissed her. "I'm a little big for that box," he whispered in her ear. "Can you tell?"

"Mac, you're forty-two years old," she scolded.

"Try telling that to my body."

"Mac!"

"Okay, don't tell it. I don't think it would pay any attention anyway."

"Hey, you guys, I don't think my first visit from Santa in ten years should be X-rated," Jessie said, wearing a playful frown.

Elizabeth held up her hand. "Listen."

There was a stillness. The snow on the roof beside Santa's sled ruffled and blew away as if something were disturbing it.

Then they heard it—bells.

"What is it?" Jessie asked.

Mac listened.

"I know," Sterling said softly. "The chapel bells are ringing. All's right with the world."

EPILOGUE

They held the wedding in the little chapel by the lake at Shangri-la on a bright May morning when the sun was shining as its golden hue rippled through the water.

"It's only appropriate that we pledge our love here," Mac said to the visitors gathered together for this special occasion. "I built a safe haven to protect and heal those who are in need. But in doing so, I turned it into a prison for my daughter and myself. Sterling came into our lives and set us free. I will love her for all my life and cherish her as my partner, my wife, and my best friend."

Sterling stood, pushed back her chair, and took her place beside Mac. "Shangri-la offers a place where those who are injured can be made whole, either physically or spiritually. I came here to be safe, without realizing that what I needed was to be made complete. Lincoln McAllister taught me that love replaces fear and that unlike some things it will last forever. I will love him for all my life and I take him to be my partner, my husband, and my best friend."

The minister placed Sterling's hand in Mac's and announced that they were now husband and wife.

When Mac kissed Sterling, all their loved ones applauded joyfully.

Then Mac reached down and lifted Sterling.

"You don't have to do that," she protested. "I can walk."

"I know, but I want to. I'll always want to hold you."

"And—"

"You'll always tell me you can do it yourself," he finished, then turned and carried her to the car. "And after little Conner and Rhett get here, I'll let you run after them all you want."

Jessie looked at Elizabeth. "Little Conner and Rhett?"

"An inside joke, darling," Conner told her.

"You never know. . . ." Elizabeth replied.

Conner put his arm around Jessie. "Too bad the doctors couldn't make it possible for Sterling to walk normally."

"She doesn't mind," Jessie assured him. "They stopped the pain. And if Daddy has anything to do with it, they'll find a way to finish the job sooner or later. If not, neither of them seems to care."

She watched her father put Sterling in the car

and close the door. Then she turned to Elizabeth and asked, "What do you know about quilts?"

"Quilts? Not much," Elizabeth said. "Why?"

"I heard Daddy talking about making one."

Conner laughed. "Was that before or after they started taking Danish lessons?"

"I don't understand my father. He's planned out the rest of their life, starting with a honeymoon in the Caribbean. Then he's building Sterling a house in Taos where she can—get this—build automobiles."

Conner shook his head. "What?"

"He said Sterling always wanted to be the head of General Motors. And you know, if she wants something, she's going to have it."

"And what's he going to do while she's becoming chairman of the board?" Burt asked.

"What else?" Jessie answered. "Make quilts."

The guests started back to the van for their return trip up the mountain, chuckling at the change in the man lovingly called the head angel.

The head angel was beaming as he carried the woman he loved into their bedroom.

"We're coming back here every year, to celebrate our anniversary, Mac. We'll have a picnic right down there on those rocks by the water—no matter what?"

"We don't have to wait for that," he said as he put her down and moved to the wall, where he punched in a new hologram. The lake and the water flashed on the screen. Overhead, a patch of moonlight cut through a black sky and frosted the scene with silver. Moments later soft music filled the room.

"It's beautiful, Mac."

"Come here, Sterling," he said, extending his hand.

She took a step toward him, placing her hand in his. "What are we doing?"

"This all started when I asked you to come to a wedding, remember?"

"Of course I remember."

"I almost got you killed."

"But you didn't. You almost died instead."

"And you saved my life."

"And you saved mine."

He nodded. "Do you remember? I asked you to save the last dance for me."

She nodded at the beautiful man whose eyes were filled with love.

"We never danced, Sterling. Dance with me now."

"Now and always," she said as she moved into his arms.

THE EDITOR'S CORNER

With these, our last LOVESWEPTs, so many thanks are in order, it's impossible to know where to start. I feel a little like those people at awards ceremonies—afraid of leaving someone off the "thank you" list.

It goes without saying that we owe our biggest thanks to the authors whose creativity, talent, and dedication set LOVESWEPT apart. As readers, you've experienced firsthand the pleasure they brought through their extraordinary writing. . . . Love stories we'll never forget, by authors we'll always remember. Nine hundred and seventeen "keepers."

Our staff underwent a few changes over the years, but one thing remained the same—our commitment to the highest standards, to a tradition of innovation and quality. Thanks go out to those who had a hand in carrying on that tradition: Carolyn Nichols, Nita Taublib, Elizabeth Barrett, Beth de Guzman, Shauna Summers, Barbara Alpert, Beverly Leung, Wendy McCurdy, Cassie Goddard, Stephanie Kip, Wendy Chen, Kara Cesare, Gina Wachtel, Carrie Feron, Tom Kleh, and David Underwood.

Special thanks go to Joy Abella. Joy often said that being an editor for LOVESWEPT was her dream job and not many people got to realize their dreams. Thanks, Joy, for helping us realize how lucky we all were to have been a part of this remarkable project. ☺

Finally, thank you, the readers, for sharing your thoughts and opinions with us. Fifteen years of LOVESWEPTs was possible only because of your loyalty and faith. We hope you will continue to look for books by your favorite authors, whom you've come to know as friends, as they move on in their writing careers. I'm sure you'll agree they are destined for great things.

With warm wishes and the hope that romance will always be a part of your lives,

Susann Brailey

Susann Brailey

Senior Editor